Renewal

Len's lips were on hers, merely brushing.
It was memory and reality blending in the spark
of a rekindled fire.

Lorna pulled away,
although it felt like denying herself
the warmth of the sun on a frigid day.

"Don't," Len said. "Please don't."

Now she was in his arms,
and he was murmuring her name
against her neck.
She was drowning in the feel of him.
Their clothes mingled in a heap on the floor.
She was ready for him,
although she did not understand how
that could have happened,
and at last she knew the bittersweet joy
of a dream fulfilled...

Carol Sturm Smith

Renewal

BALLANTINE BOOKS • NEW YORK

Library of Congress Catalog Card Number: 81-22892
ISBN 0-345-29755-5

Manufactured in the United States of America

First Edition: July 1982

For Pam and Chuck, who helped bring Wes back into my life

Chapter One

"LORNA! LORNA WILLIS! WELL, I'LL BE!"

Lorna Willis Robinson hadn't heard Len Gold's voice in twenty years. His rich baritone seemed slightly lower in pitch, but the timbre hadn't changed. Neither had his wicked smile, which still made laughing lights dance in his dark eyes. He was heavier now by a few pounds, Lorna judged, and he was wearing his thick brown hair longer than he had in high school. He had always been nice-looking and maturity agreed with him. He was more than good-looking now. He was beautifully handsome.

"Hello, Len," Lorna said.

"How are you? How have you been? What are you doing?" Len laughed. "There's so much to say, so much to ask—I don't know where to begin!"

"Yes," Lorna said. "Yes. I know. I know what you mean." She pulled her eyes away from Len's face, aware that he had glanced at her left hand where she no longer wore the wedding band that had been on her finger for nearly fifteen years. She forced herself to look down at the glass cabinet behind which she stood, the cabinet that held the selection of fine pens and pencils carried by Willet's, the stationery store she had managed for the past two years.

But she could not help herself; she looked up again, first to reassure herself that Len was really

1

standing on the other side of the counter, then at the ring finger of his left hand.

He was wearing a plain, narrow, gold band that showed signs of long wear.

"Yes," Len said. "I'm married. Have been for nearly fifteen years. And you?"

"Divorced," Lorna said, the word still not feeling comfortable even though she had said it dozens of times during the past twelve months. "A year ago. I was married for nearly fifteen years, too."

"Children?" Len asked.

"Two," Lorna said. "Cindy's twelve, and Daniel's going to be nine next month."

"I have three," Len said. "All boys. The oldest is eleven, and we've got twins who are eight."

"That's nice," Lorna said.

"Roger, Robert and Richard."

"Very alliterative," Lorna said, surprised at the sense of turmoil she was feeling.

"Yes, I tried to talk Margot out of it, but she insisted."

Margot, Lorna thought to herself. He married Margot Skillen! She always had wanted him, even when he was chasing after me!

"Look," Len said, "I assume you're working here, because you're on the other side of the counter—"

"I manage the store."

Len nodded as if that piece of information made perfect sense to him, as if somehow he seemed to have known that today was the day they were to meet again after all these years, as if the errand that had brought him into the store had deserved a

2

reward like the prize in a Crackerjack box. Lorna, however, was flustered; in all of the fantasies she had had over the years that involved seeing Len again, not one had been as simple as this unexpected meeting.

"I need a birthday present for the son of some friends of ours," Len said. "I thought I'd get him a good pen."

"Well, you came to the right place," Lorna said, automatically smiling her best saleslady smile.

Len laughed. "No need for that," he said. "A Parker's a Parker. Do you have one with cartridges for about twenty dollars?"

"Sure," Lorna said, sliding open the glass door, pulling out a case and placing it on the black velveteen presentation stand. She took the cover from the box and removed the pen.

Len shook his head. "That's fine," he said.

"Is the color all right? We also have this model in maroon and blue, I think." Lorna started to check the stock in the drawer below the cabinet, but Len stopped her. "No. Don't bother," he said. "I'll take this one. And extra cartridges, too."

"Black? Blue? Green?"

"An assortment. You pick them out."

"Okay," Lorna said, making a selection from the hooks that held the refills. She placed them on the counter. "Do you need anything else?"

"No. Just let me know what the damage is."

"Cash or charge?"

"Cash."

Lorna figured the sales tax, added it to the price of the pen and cartridges, hesitated for a moment, and then decided not to ask Len for his address for their mailing list—the normal procedure for cash sales.

"Would you—could you take a break for a little while?" Len said. "It's a beautiful day. We could take a walk or have some coffee." As if realizing that she needed a bit of time to make a decision, Len reached over and picked up the pen. He replaced it in the box and handed it to Lorna. "Would it be possible to get this gift-wrapped?"

"Sure," Lorna said. "That's Gail behind the register. She'll gift-wrap it for you after you pay her." And then, on an impulse, because she could not think of any reason not to, Lorna decided to go with the moment. "Give me a couple of minutes," she said. "I have a few calls to make before I can leave."

The look of delight on Len's face was momentarily frightening to Lorna. It was as if the years that had passed since she had last seen him had never happened—as if she were still in her teens, still a virgin. She experienced a surge of the feelings that had haunted her then, feelings that had made her afraid of her own body, feelings that had caused her torment to a degree she had never again experienced—feelings that her romance with Len had caused—feelings that had, in the end, made her break up with him. Even as *that* thought crossed her mind, Lorna realized there had been times during this year of living alone, after her divorce from Philip, when her sexual desires had been as strong as those she experienced as a teenager. The difference was that the feelings were not forbidden now. She recognized them for what they were, and that knowledge made it easier for her to handle them.

"Lorna."

With a start Lorna realized that she had been daydreaming, that perhaps half a minute had gone by during which she had been staring at the sales pad before her on the counter. Hastily, she tore the sales slip free from the pad and handed it to Len. "I'm okay," she said. "I was just thinking . . . just remembering."

"I know," Len said. "Go take care of your business, and then we can spend some time remembering together." He took the sales slip and the pen and headed for the cashier.

Lorna walked quickly to the stockroom at the back of the store. She checked her watch. It was just after three o'clock, too early for Cindy and Daniel to be home from school. Lorna shook her head in dismay. Whatever had made her think that she had to call her children to say that she would be home late? She gathered her purse and sweater, then headed for the bathroom to repair her makeup to make it seem as if she had had things to attend to although she did not. For the last few weeks business had been very slow—so slow, in fact, that Lorna was worried Mr. Willet might tell her to let one of the salespeople go. It was not a prospect that gave her pleasure. Once before she had had to fire someone; the worry before and the guilt after the act had bothered her for weeks.

With a conscious effort, Lorna forced herself to relax and checked her reflection in the mirror over the sink. Her large brown eyes, her best feature, naturally lined with long lashes, looked back at her steadily. She did not like the signs of tension that the past two years—her separation and divorce from Philip—had etched on her face, but Len's unexpected appearance had caused a blush of color to appear on her high cheekbones, and a sense of excitement and animation showed. Taking her time, Lorna put on fresh lipstick, then vigorously brushed her dark brown hair. She still wore it falling free, slightly below shoulder-length. Recently she had begun having her hair rinsed to tend to the gray. Slowly, she pulled her hair up and back from her face, holding it in place the way barrettes had when she was younger—when she was seventeen years old and Len Gold's girl friend.

Unexpectedly, a laugh broke free. What an unbecoming hair style she had worn through most of high school, although she had not realized it at the time and Len had never commented on it. Lorna let her hair fall back into place, shaking her head to give it a bit of bounce, then straightened the collar of her pink-and-purple silk print blouse. It was her favorite blouse, one she reserved for days when she needed something a little special to get her moving in the morning. Now she was glad the day had started out slowly for her, because she knew the blouse was flattering.

Satisfied, Lorna returned her lipstick and brush to her pocketbook and headed back to the main part of the store. Len was waiting for her outside the store, which was located on Forty-sixth Street in Manhattan, a few blocks west of Fifth Avenue.

"I'm going out for a while, Gail," she said to the middle-aged woman behind the register, a part-time employee who had been with the store for less than half a year. Gail was a widow in her early fifties who needed the job, the woman Lorna would have to fire if business did not pick up. "Can you cover for me?"

"Sure," Gail said, her eyes automatically turning to assess Len, who was looking at the display in the front window.

"An old friend," Lorna said hastily. "From high school days. We haven't seen each other in years." Almost twenty years, to be exact, Lorna thought. Twenty years this coming February.

"He's very attractive," Gail said.

"And married, too," Lorna said, annoyed with herself for making the remark. She slung her sweater over her shoulders and headed for the door.

Chapter Two

No, HE ISN'T ATTRACTIVE, LORNA THOUGHT, AS Len took her arm and guided them down the street, heading for Sixth Avenue—he's handsome. He always had had a bit of the rogue about him but as a teenager, he was gangly. Age had given him polish, and he was very well dressed in a dark three-piece suit, nicely burnished gray cordovans, and a foulard tie with a pattern that was predominantly dark green, exactly the color of his eyes. His leather briefcase was an expensive one with brass fittings, well worn but well taken care of also, showing the care with which saddle soap was regularly applied.

"What do you do for a living?" Lorna said. "I pretty much dropped out of touch with everyone except my mother after I went away to school."

"Yes, I know," Len said. "I see old friends every now and then and I always ask about you."

"That didn't answer my question."

"I'm in publishing," Len said. "Not the end of things I wanted when I was younger, although I did study journalism in college. I was just made general manager of the trade book division of Brockton and Company."

Lorna laughed, unable to help herself.

"What's so funny about that?" Len said. "Brockton's one of the largest publishing companies in the country, and I've worked my way up very fast."

"I know," Lorna said. "Our birthdays are less than a year apart."

"Are you going to tell me what made you laugh?" Len asked.

"Philip Robinson."

"Right. He's a Brockton author. Writes good mystery stories. I just finished reading galleys of his new book, *Clear Lake*. I agree with the editorial department that he's finally going to hit the best-seller lists with this one. It's about time. We've published five or six books of his."

"Six," Lorna said. "The new one will make seven."

"So, you're one of his fans. That's good to know. I like his books, too. Besides growing up in Buffalo, it gives us another thing in common."

"He's my ex-husband," Lorna said.

They stopped at the corner of Sixth Avenue to wait for the light, and there was a pause in the conversation as Len absorbed this piece of information.

"I was at the publication parties for both of Philip Robinson's last books," Len said. "You weren't there."

"No. We were already . . . we were in the process of separating when *Cool, Dark and Deadly* was published. And Daniel was sick the time before. He's asthmatic."

"I'm sorry," Len said. "Our neighbors' daughter has asthma, and it's worrisome, isn't it."

"Yes," Lorna said, "but Daniel seems to be growing out of it a bit now."

"I'm glad."

The light changed and they crossed the avenue, continuing on Forty-sixth Street. Len pointed to a stationery store across the street. "You can thank a salesgirl in there for our meeting," he said. "She was so rude I walked out of the store."

"Are you in the neighborhood often?"

"Occasionally. My office is uptown—"

"I know," Lorna said.

"Yes, of course. But there are a few restaurants around here I like, and. . . ." Len broke off and stopped, turning to look at Lorna.

Somehow, over the years, Lorna realized, the visual image she held of Len in her memory had never altered. She had made no allowance for the passage of time. When she thought of him she thought of the Len she had known during the years they had been the steadiest couple in their crowd, the years during which they had sung together, learned how to play pool, read the same books, spent as much time together as they could to the exclusion of other relationships.

Lorna laughed. "You know. I just realized that you're wearing glasses!" she said. "Isn't that strange?"

Len shrugged and took them off, placing them in the case he carried in his inside jacket pocket. "Usually I wear them only in the office or for reading," he said, "but recently I've been forgetting to take them off."

"And you still turn your head to the side a bit when you're looking at me."

Len reached for Lorna's hand and bent to kiss the back of it lightly. "That's because I don't quite believe I'm seeing you in the flesh," he said. Then he increased the pressure on her hand and began to walk more quickly, still heading east.

"Where are we going?" Lorna asked.

"Just come on," Len said.

"Where?"

"I'm taking you to the Oyster Bar at Grand Central Station."

"Whatever for?" Lorna said.

"Because I want to buy you some oysters and a lobster."

"A lobster! That's ridiculous. I'm not hungry. It's half past three, in the middle of the afternoon and I had lunch just. . . ." Lorna stopped, a blush that seemed to start at her toes beginning to make its way through her body. She pulled her hand away from Len's and stopped walking so suddenly that a man walking behind them bumped into her, jostling her pocketbook from her shoulder.

Len bent to retrieve it. His smile showed his dimples; Lorna was glad that he hadn't laughed, that he didn't comment on the flush she was sure showed on her face.

And then she laughed again. "I think about that weekend sometimes," she said then. "It rates high on my list of all-time embarrassments."

"We were both pretty young, Lorna," Len said. "I was embarrassed, too. I've learned a lot since then."

"Haven't we all?" Lorna said. "Haven't we all?"

They ended up sitting on the steps of the Public Library on Fifth Avenue at Forty-second Street. Neither of them was ready to talk about the weekend that had put an end to their romance, yet both were aware of memories surfacing. Each knew that the other was thinking of that weekend. The afternoon sun was warm on this late October day, an Indian summer day, and soon Lorna removed her sweater, folded it neatly and placed it on her lap.

"What was the name of that restaurant, do you remember?" Len asked.

"The Schelling Family's Surf Maid," Lorna said, "although there sure wasn't any surf anywhere near around." She paused for a moment, then added, "The motel was called 'The DeVille,' and the room had light beige plaster walls with cracks, a television set that flickered, and a white quilt with big red-and-yellow flowers on the bed. None of the furniture matched. It was functional, but very strange."

"Right," Len said. "That's right."

"Philip and I lived near the ocean for a while, right after we got married. In New Jersey. I liked it. A lot. But. . . ."

"What happened?"

"Philip," Lorna said. She shrugged. "He missed New York. I liked the idea of moving into Manhattan also, but now I wish we hadn't sold the house. I would have taken the kids back there to live. Philip never wanted me to take a job, and we spent the money we made on the house sale supporting ourselves. Philip never even earned out his small advances on the first few books, and . . . well, you know. Most people think that you publish a book and you're automatically rich. It just doesn't work that way."

"I know," Len said. "You don't have to tell me. I'm in the business. But he's over the hurdle now. There should be quite a bit of money coming from the new novel."

"I hope so. The kids . . . Cindy's nearly a teen-ager, and Daniel has a real bookworm tendency. He doesn't even really know how to play baseball. It would have been better for them, I think, to have been reared outside of Manhattan."

Len looked at Lorna intensely for a moment, started to say something, and then changed his mind. He leaned back against the concrete, placed his elbows on the step behind him, stretching out his legs and crossing his ankles. On the other side of the handrail, sitting several steps below them, a woman in a floral print dress was also taking the sun, holding a metallic reflector against her neck.

Len nodded in her direction. "That looks like some kind of a Martian growth she's got there."

"Nope. It's definitely a Venusian goiter," Lorna said, glad that Len had opened the door for making the mood lighter. Her worries about Cindy had been weighing heavily on her recently, but that wasn't Len's problem.

"Are you sure?"

"Absolutely positive," Lorna said. "Everyone knows that Martians are notorious for picking on people who are thin and wiry. She's definitely—"

Len's hands were on her shoulders then, turning her around to face him, the warmth of his touch seeping through the fabric of her blouse, and the look in his eyes, eyes now the black-green of surf pounding against rocks on a stormy day, nearly took her breath away.

"We have unfinished business, Lorna. You know that, don't you," he said.

"Don't, Len, please."

"But it's true. I know it, and you know it, too, if you're anywhere near as honest with yourself as you used to be. We're not kids now, and. . . ."

The kiss Lorna felt was in her memory, but the desire was of the here-and-now, of the instant, the moment. With an effort of will, she turned her face away, toward the street, the noise of the traffic on Fifth Avenue suddenly making sense to her, reminding her of where she was. On the street below the library steps, the pedestrians were more numerous than they had been just a short while before.

"It's nearly rush hour," Lorna said. "I've got to get back to Willet's. There are things I have to do."

"Lorna—"

"No," she said. "Please don't, Len. Sometimes business stays unfinished because that's the way it's meant to be."

Momentarily Len tightened his grip on Lorna's shoulders, but just as suddenly he removed his hands and reached for his briefcase.

"Okay," he said. "Is it all right if I walk you back to the store?"

"No, I don't think so." Lorna reached for her sweater, still feeling Len's touch, glad that he had released her yet wanting more. She got to her feet and held out her hand. "It was nice to see you, Len. Give my best . . . give my best to Margot. Is she well?"

"She's fine," Len said. "And you don't mean that at all. You and Margot never liked each other."

Lorna shrugged and slowly let her arm fall to her side. Len was still reclining on the steps, and he obviously had no intention of ending this meeting by shaking hands.

"I've got to go," Lorna said.

"Okay."

She walked down a few steps, then stopped and turned.

Len was watching her.

"You're going to dream about me tonight, Lorna," he said.

She shrugged. "Maybe," she said.

"No 'maybe,'" he said. "You are."

Lorna turned away, walking down the rest of the steps, suddenly angry, and by the time she reached the corner she was running, pushing her way through hordes of strangers making their way home for the evening.

Chapter Three

"GOOD EVENING, SAM," LORNA SAID TO THE whitehaired uniformed doorman of her apartment building on East Thirty-fifth Street in the Murray Hill residential section of Manhattan.

"Hello, Mrs. Robinson. I have a package for you. I gave the rest of the mail to Daniel when he got home from school, but I forgot to give him the package."

"No problem," Lorna said. She walked to the back end of the half-mirrored lobby, her heels echoing on the marble floor, and rang for the elevator while waiting for Sam to retrieve the package from the mailroom. The lobby clock read 7:14. It was nearly forty-five minutes later than she usually got home, but it had been a flurry of last-minute customers at Willet's and not her excursion with Len that was responsible.

"Here you are," Sam said, handing her a flat package that looked as if it contained an oversized book. It was from her mother.

"Thanks, Sam," Lorna said.

"Mrs. Robinson, Mr. Robinson's upstairs. You asked me to let you know—"

"Right," Lorna said. "Thanks for the warning."

The battle for the apartment had been a bitter one. Lorna and Philip had lived in the building for almost ten years when they separated, and Philip had written five of his novels in the office he had set up in one of the rooms that overlooked the East River. Daniel had never known another home, although Cindy could remember the house on the New Jersey shore, vague memories that she spoke about wistfully.

In the end, so far as the apartment was concerned, Lorna's argument that the break in itself was traumatic enough for the children without their moving as well had turned the tide in her favor. Philip's worry that he would not be able to write without his office had proved false. The office was a den now, where the children could watch television with their friends or play. And Philip's last two books, written in the apartment he had taken on the upper West Side, had been no more difficult for him than the earlier ones except for the changes in his routine that had to do with the divorce. He had taken his beloved oiled oak rolltop desk, his well-worn leather swivel chair, and other familiar working tools with him when he moved out.

Taken everything but Sally Thornton, Lorna thought—the woman who lived on the penthouse floor, the divorcée with whom Philip had begun an affair shortly after Lorna had found the job at Willet's.

16

Lorna entered the elevator, pushed the button for the fourteenth floor, and found herself wondering why Philip was upstairs. On several occasions during the past few months she had arrived home to find Philip there, his excuse always being that he wanted to see the children. Lorna stopped herself—it *wasn't* an excuse, she knew. Philip's love for Cindy and Daniel was real, and there was no doubt in Lorna's mind that Philip continued to suffer greatly from the loss of the children in his day-to-day life.

She looked at the package in her hands, wondering what it could be. Her mother was an erratic letter-writer, but nearly every month a package arrived, always addressed to Lorna but usually containing something for Cindy or Daniel. To avoid problems, Lorna never opened the packages, always letting the children have that pleasure. Although the little gifts almost always arrived one at a time, Mildred was quite good about alternating, and Cindy and Daniel had grown used to taking turns. This one was undoubtedly for Cindy.

Lorna took her keys from her purse when the elevator stopped, walked down the hall, unlocked and entered the apartment.

The television was blaring in the den. Philip was sitting in the wingback chair near the living room windows, his arms crossed against his chest, his left leg crossed over his right. His sandy blond hair had been cut since Lorna had seen him the week before, although it was still slightly long at the nape, the way he liked it. He was wearing a dark rust button-front wool sweater she had never seen. He was a handsome man, Philip Robinson,

17

with a distinguished air. He looked like a man who might be an author or an actor—a man who would not be content with a nine-to-five life.

"Hello, Philip," she said. "Sam told me you were here."

Philip looked at his watch. "You're late."

"Yes, I know. We had not one but three last-minute customers."

"I fed the kids. Cindy's downstairs with Dawn."

"Okay. Thanks."

Lorna tossed the package from her mother on the little gateleg hallway table and hung her cardigan in the closet. There had been a mild trace of censure in Philip's tone, but she wasn't about to respond to it. There was always an adequate supply of food in the apartment—things that both Cindy and Daniel could handle on nights when she was late. While it was true that when she first returned to work it had been over Philip's strong protests, there was now no choice as to whether she worked or not. Philip knew that as well as she did. Their divorce had carried with it a provision for child-support payments, but Lorna received no alimony, and she needed the money she was paid for her work at Willet's.

"What brings you around?" Lorna asked, heading for the small, efficient kitchen to get her own supper ready. The bottle of vodka was on the kitchen counter—Philip had obviously made himself a drink.

"I was wondering if it would be all right if we switched weekends around," Philip said. He came and stood in the doorway of the kitchen; the glass in his hand was nearly empty.

"Would you like a refill?" Lorna asked.

"Okay," Philip said. "I'll bring you a bottle next time I come."

"Fine," Lorna said. She refreshed Philip's drink, hesitated, then made herself a screwdriver. She was still feeling jumpy from her encounter with Len, and Philip's presence in the apartment did not help at all.

"Tough day?" Philip asked. "You usually don't drink during the week."

Lorna shrugged. "Nothing in particular," she said. "I just thought I'd join you."

Philip raised his glass. Lorna hesitated for a moment, then responded with her own.

"I've been invited to Ben's place weekend after next, and he's going to have his kids. I'm sure Daniel and Cindy would like to go if it's all right with you," Philip said.

"Oh. Sure. That's okay. They'll be very pleased," Lorna said, feeling a pang of regret. She turned to the refrigerator and began to assemble her dinner so that Philip would not notice her reaction. Ben Ditman, who was Philip's editor at Brockton, had a lovely country home in Connecticut, set back from the road on a dirt lane in a beautiful wooded area. Formerly, he had invited all of them for weekends several times a year. Lorna had never met Ben's wife—they had been divorced before Ben took Philip on as one of his writers—but Ben had always timed his invitations to coincide with weekends when he had custody of his children, who were nearly the same ages as Cindy and Daniel. Lorna liked Ben, but she had not seen him since her divorce from Philip, and knew that she probably would not see him again. There were other pople—too many other people —who had been a part of her life only because they were part of Philip's life, and Lorna had barely begun to fill that terrible gap.

"I bumped into an old friend today," Lorna said then.

"Oh?"

"Len," she said. "Len Gold."

"The guy you used to date in high school?"

"The one and the same," Lorna said, deliberately keeping her back turned toward Philip. She put a small amount of water in the bottom of her five-quart Revere Ware pot, fit her bamboo steamer in place and spooned a portion of the casserole she had made for dinner the night before into a flat ceramic bowl to heat.

She hesitated, then asked, "Are you hungry?"

"A little," Philip said. "The kids wanted TV dinners, but I spotted that and it looked good. I'll join you, if you don't mind."

"No, that's fine," Lorna said. And, in fact, she was glad, because tonight, if Philip had not been there, she probably would have eaten the casserole cold, not bothering to put together an adequate dinner for herself. She added another portion to the bowl, poured additional water into the pot, and turned on the gas.

"I'll help," Philip said.

"Okay. Do you want to do a salad?"

"Sure." He opened the refrigerator. "What was it like, seeing him?" Philip's tone was so deliberately casual that it caused Lorna to look around at him for a visual clue to his mood. Philip's was an open face, usually mirroring his mood quite accurately, but his back was turned as he rummaged in the refrigerator for the salad greens.

"It was strange seeing him," Lorna said. "Very strange."

"In what way?"

"Oh, I don't know. Physically, the years show, but still, it was . . . it was as if the years hadn't passed. As if they didn't matter, somehow."

"Still sexy, eh?"

Lorna laughed. "You sounded jealous just then, Philip," she said.

Philip turned to look at her. "You used to talk about him a lot, Lorna."

"I did?"

"Yes, you did."

Lorna shrugged. "I guess so."

"Sometimes I think his presence in our lives was more of an influence on our marriage going sour than my affair with Sally Thornton."

"You can't be serious!"

Philip shrugged. "Maybe not," he said.

They were silent then, working together in the kitchen as they had done so many times before, adjusting to give each other the room they needed out of long habit.

"I haven't even said hello to Daniel," Lorna said once everything was under control. "I'd better do that before we get settled at the table."

"Go ahead," Philip said. "I'll take care of the dishes and silverware."

"Thanks."

Daniel was sprawled on the blue tweed sofa bed in the den, his feet dangling over the arm. His sneakers were still on, although both sets of laces were untied. His light brown hair, which he wore even longer than Philip's, fell across his forehead. He was asleep, despite the sound of the television, which was very loud. His schoolbooks were on the floor by his side, his completed homework papers neatly arranged on top. Unlike Cindy, who had to be prodded to do her homework, Daniel displayed an almost adult resignation about his studying; although Lorna could never understand how he was able to do his work with the television on, she did not bother him about it.

She kissed her son lightly on the forehead, turned down the volume on the television set, then returned to the kitchen.

"He's sound asleep," she said.

"He said he was tired earlier," Philip said. "Has he been feeling all right?"

"Fine," Lorna said. "He was up late last night, though. There was a movie he wanted to see, and I let him. What time did Cindy say she'd be home?"

"Nine."

"Okay."

They settled themselves at the round oak table in the dining area—Lorna had not had any occasion to use the leaves that opened the table to seat twelve since the separation and divorce. Much to her surprise, because she had thought she was hungry, she found herself picking at her food. "He works for Brockton," she said then. "He's the manager of the trade book division."

"Who?"

"Len. That's what he told me. He said . . . he said he met you at both of your last publication parties."

"I don't remember," Philip said. "I'm sure I

would have . . . Marsh," he said. "He calls him-self 'Marsh' Gold."

Lorna nodded. "That's right. I'd forgotten. 'Marsh' is a family name. It was his grandfather's, but he hated it and used his middle name instead. The kids used to call him 'Marshmallow' until he got everyone to call him 'Len.'"

The expression on Philip's face was one that Lorna did not understand; there was annoyance there; and something else, too.

"He's a very nice-looking man," Philip said. "It's really a coincidence, isn't it?"

"Yes, I used to wonder what had become of him," Lorna agreed.

An awkward silence fell between them, a si-lence Lorna suddenly recognized as a silence similar to the ones that had happened between them soon after their divorce, when Philip had, on occasion, talked openly about Sally Thornton. Although he had no longer been seeing the woman, for a long time Lorna blamed her for the breakup of their marriage.

Philip finished his food and pushed his plate away. "That was good," he said. "Thanks."

"You're welcome. Would you like dessert? There's fruit or chocolate ice cream."

"No, thanks."

"Coffee?"

"Okay."

Philip helped her clear the table; then they did the dishes while waiting for the coffee water to boil.

"Are you going to see him again?" Philip asked.

"I don't know," Lorna said, although she real-ized that she, too, had been wondering about that

23

possibility. "And even if I did, it doesn't matter. He's married."

"I was married when I started seeing Sally," Philip said, a remark that was delivered in a hard icy tone of voice that indicated great anger seething in him.

Chapter Four

LORNA STARTED TO RESPOND, BUT JUST THEN THE front door opened and Cindy burst into the apartment.

"Dad, you're still here!" she said. "Hi, Mom!" Cindy hugged Lorna, kissed her on one cheek, kissed Philip on both of his, helped herself to a mouthful of leftover casserole, and then a second on which she sprinkled salt—she was like a whirlwind of energy in the little kitchen, for just as suddenly as she had entered she blew them both kisses and headed for the den, stopping in front of the hall mirror to toss her shoulder-length honey blond hair back and to pull her long-sleeved blue T-shirt down over the waistband of her baggy khaki pants. This action showed quite clearly that Cindy was developing, although she still had not matured. That fact was not lost on Philip either, and Lorna and he exchanged glances, the glances of parents proud yet concerned about a nearly adolescent daughter, a mutual concern that the purely legal business of divorce could never sever.

"Hey, yippee-doo!" Cindy shrieked, stopping as she noticed the package from her grandmother on the hall table. She grabbed it and ripped the Jiffy bag open like a six-year-old confronted with a surprise birthday present. Her reaction unexpectedly brought a lump to Lorna's throat. What an enigma her daughter was on the verge of becoming—still a child and yet almost not a child. . . .

Surprisingly, making the first move of intimacy either of them had attempted since their divorce, Philip reached out and took Lorna's hand. He gave it a firm squeeze before letting go so quickly Lorna wondered if she had imagined the moment —the way earlier in the day she had remembered the feel of Len's kiss.

"Hey, Mom, there's a letter here for you from Grandma," Cindy said. She held it up for Lorna to see before grasping it between her teeth for safekeeping, while she ripped layers of pink tissue paper away from what was indeed a book, as Lorna had surmised in the elevator.

"Don't drop the tissue on the floor, Cindy," Lorna said.

Cindy took the letter from her mouth and walked slowly towards the kitchen. "I'll pick it up, Mom, don't worry," she said. Absently, she handed the letter to Lorna. She was looking at the book with a puzzled expression. She opened the cover. "You know, I don't think this is for me. I think it's for you, Mom. What do you think?" She handed the book over to Lorna also.

It was Lorna's high school yearbook, a coincidence which, in light of her meeting with Len earlier in the day, was quite impossible for Lorna to comprehend. She hefted the yearbook and shook her head in anguished bemusement.

"Open this for me, will you, Cindy-Bear?" she said, handing the letter back to her daughter.

"What is that, Mom?" Cindy asked, tearing open the envelope flap.

"It's your Mom's yearbook," Philip said. He also recognized the book that Lorna's mother had pulled out for him to look at during the first weekend Lorna had brought him home while they were courting.

"Really!" Cindy said. "Is there a picture of you, Mom?"

"Sure," Lorna said.

"Hey, let me see." Cindy took the book from Lorna and gave her the letter.

"Mildred sure has a special sense of timing, doesn't she?" Philip commented.

"That she does," Lorna agreed.

The letter was short, just a few lines:

Lorna, dear:

I was cleaning out closets today and came across this. I thought it was time for you to have it. I saw your friend Marilen the other day, and she asked about you. She and Michael are still happily married, and have had another baby. She was very sorry to hear about your divorce, but I felt it was necessary to tell her.

26

Please write or call to let me know that you've received this.

Love,
Mother

"God," Lorna said, handing the note to Philip. "I haven't seen Marilen since I left Buffalo, and it sounds like Mother still hasn't gotten used to the idea that we're divorced."

"She probably never will," Philip said. "You can't change that, Lorna. She has old-fashioned values, but there's nothing wrong with that. It's one of the things I always liked about Mildred."

"Yes, I know. But in her case, 'old-fashioned' almost equates with 'Puritan,' and—"

"Yikes! Look at you!" Cindy said. She had found Lorna's picture in the yearbook. Despite herself, Lorna moved closer to her daughter and looked over her shoulder. She had always hated the picture in the yearbook—the disastrous haircut she had gotten the week before the photo was taken, the serious look, the half-closed eyes, the unflattering sweater . . . she laughed.

"It's still as awful as I remembered," she said.

". . . chorus and glee club. Gee, you didn't do much, did you, Mom?" Cindy said, looking at the activities listings under other pictures in the book.

"No," Lorna said. "I studied and sang." And spent time with Len, she thought.

"Right. I knew that, you told me," Cindy said. "But I guess it's different seeing it in print."

"Enough," Lorna said then, taking the yearbook from Cindy.

"Hey, I'm not done looking yet!" Cindy said.

"Tomorrow, Cindy. It's getting late. Do you have homework?"

"I did it downstairs at Dawn's."

"Okay. Then take your shower and get ready for bed."

"Gee, Mom, it's still early."

"It's nearly ten," Philip said, checking his watch. He looked at Lorna. "Daniel's still asleep?"

"Yes, I guess so."

"I'll check."

Lorna gave the kitchen a final glance, flipped out the light, and took the yearbook into the bedroom for safekeeping. It seemed strange to her now to be in the bedroom she had shared with Philip when he was in the apartment, so she returned to the living room quickly.

"Daniel is still asleep," Philip said.

"That's okay," Lorna said. "Might as well just let him stay where he is, on the sofa bed."

"I'll get a blanket for him," Philip said. He made a move towards Daniel's room, then stopped. "Is that okay?"

"Sure," Lorna said.

A half hour later, showered and with her hair in soft rubber curlers, Cindy came to kiss them good night. She stood in the hallway for a moment before going into her room.

"It's nice to see you both here," she said, then hastily retired before either one of them could tell her not to bring that subject up again.

"Would you like another cup of coffee?" Lorna offered.

"No, it's getting late," Philip said.

"A brandy?"

Philip hesitated, then shook his head. "No. I think I had better be going," he said. "I made a good start on the new book over the weekend."

"Len said he's read galleys on *Clear Lake,* and that Brockton's going to publish in the spring. They think you're going to hit the best-seller lists this time."

"I hope so, but I'll believe that when I see it." He retrieved his jacket from the hall closet and headed for the door. "I'll pick the kids up as soon as they get home from school next Friday," he said, "and I'll have them back Sunday night."

"Fine," Lorna said.

Philip hesitated at the door. Lorna had come to stand next to him, waiting to lock the door behind him. He reached out and placed his hand lightly on her cheek. "Do you ever think we made a mistake, Lorna?" he asked.

She shrugged. "Sometimes."

"Are you very lonely?"

"I have the kids."

"I know. But that's not the same, is it?"

"No," she said honestly. "No. It's not."

For a split second, Lorna thought that Philip was going to kiss her, but he didn't.

And then he was gone.

She closed and locked the apartment door, took a quick look around the living room to make sure that things were in place, then headed for the bedroom, unbuttoning her blouse and beginning to undress for bed. Hastily, she pulled on her nightgown, turned down the sheets, and flipped on the bedside light.

The yearbook on the dresser was irresistible,

but just as irresistible was the silence of the night that seemed to fill the room now that she was alone for the first time that day. She crawled into bed, drew the soft blue-and-white-flowered sheet and the light rose blanket up around her chin, and settled back against the down pillow. Crossing her arms above her head, Lorna thought about the yearbook, names of old friends—names she had not thought about in years—surfacing in her thoughts. At the edges of her mind, she could feel the first tinglings of the excitement she knew she would let herself feel tonight. The memories were already beginning to crowd in on her, the fantasy dreams that would come—that were already there full-blown when, for an instant, she closed her eyes—thoughts of Len, of the Len she had known in her past and the Len who had so unexpectedly appeared now as part of her present . . . and thoughts of Philip, too.

Lorna opened her eyes and looked around the bedroom at the familiar white provincial furniture, the pictures of Cindy and Daniel on the dresser, the soft blue-gray curtains at the windows, reassuring herself that she was safe, safe here in the place she called home. Then she reached over, flicked out the bedside light, snuggled down, and closed her eyes again—and, as Len had predicted, she began to dream.

Chapter Five

"HOW DO YOU DO IT, LORNA?" BETH PILSNER said. "Your apartment is always clean and you've got two kids, not one, and a full-time job." Beth Pilsner helped herself to a second cup of coffee and watched as Lorna finished washing the last of the breakfast dishes. Saturday morning breakfast and shopping for the week's groceries was standard procedure for Lorna and Beth, who lived with her daughter, Dawn, on the eleventh floor of the building. From the den came the quarrelsome voices of Cindy and Daniel fighting for control of the television, a fight which Daniel invariably lost when Dawn, Cindy's best friend, was also in the apartment.

"You ask that every Saturday, Beth," Lorna said, "even when we're at your place."

Beth chuckled. "I guess I do," she said. "Sometimes, you make me feel guilty because you're so organized."

"I don't have any choice," Lorna said.

"Sure you do, my friend. You could be a compulsive slob like I am."

"You're too hard on yourself, Beth. Your place is always perfectly clean."

"Sure. I've got a rich ex-husband who pays me

enough alimony so I can afford a professional cleaning service three times a week."

"Well, I certainly envy you that. I'm good about keeping up the kitchen and living room and my bedroom, but Daniel's and Cindy's rooms are disaster areas. Let's not talk about it today, okay?"

"Okay." Beth retrieved her purse and headed for the hallway mirror to check her hair and makeup. She was an attractive woman, a few years younger than Lorna, with honey blond hair almost exactly the color of Cindy's and large brown eyes that had a tendency to look mournful. Once Beth had confided to Lorna that she liked having friends who were bigger-boned and taller than she was. Beth was just five feet two inches tall and weighed barely a hundred pounds. Her remark had made Lorna laugh because it had been delivered in a solemn tone which Beth usually reserved for her rare comments about current events.

"You know, a funny thing happened earlier this week," Lorna said then.

"Oh?"

"An old friend of mine came into Willet's. Someone I hadn't seen in nearly twenty years."

"A man?"

"Yes."

"Oh, good," Beth said. "Come on." She walked back into the kitchen and took the terry-cloth dish towel from Lorna, tucking it into the white ceramic ring near the sink. "Leave the dishes," she said. "They'll dry by themselves. Let's go. I want to hear all about it."

Lorna laughed. "That's all there is," she said. "There's nothing else to tell."

"Don't be silly. Of course, there's more. If there wasn't more, you would have called immediately to tell me instead of waiting like this. I know you, Lorna. When things are important you always churn them around for a while in that rational brain of yours before you talk about them."

"Am I that transparent?"

"Yes." Beth's answer was so swift and affirmative that Lorna was momentarily taken aback.

"Well, I'm glad I put off my call to Mildred then," she said.

"Why?"

"Oh, there was one of those funny coincidences that happen every now and then," Lorna explained. "The day Len came into the store I received a letter and a package from mother—it was my high school yearbook. She asked me to call when I received it, but I haven't yet."

"I don't understand," Beth said.

"Len. Len Gold. I was heavily involved with him for a couple of years when we were teenagers. Mildred wanted me to marry him, but. . . ."

"Go on."

Lorna shrugged. "Okay," she said. "I might as well get it off my chest. I've been thinking about him a lot these past few days. I'm sorry the meeting happened. He's married, and he's still attractive . . . no, he's more than attractive, he's one of the handsomest men I've ever seen. If things had worked out differently, we might have been married, and I was scared to death of the sexual feelings he made me feel when I was younger. The meeting's been making me go through those awful 'what would have happened if' kinds of things. I haven't been sleeping well."

"Are you going to see him again?"

"I don't know," Lorna said.

"Do you want to?"

"I don't know that either."

Beth checked her watch. "Hey, come on," she said. "We can talk while we shop. If we don't get going, we're going to hit the noon crowd."

"Okay." Lorna took her soft boxer-cut suede jacket from the closet, let the children know that she and Beth were leaving, then they headed for the supermarket.

It was a beautiful, sunny fall day, the air crisp and unusually clean for New York, reminiscent of the day Len had come into the store, although a bit more chilly. As usual, Lorna and Beth walked the few blocks more or less in silence, stopping now and then to window-shop.

The window display had been changed in a clothing store where Lorna shopped occasionally, so she paused for a minute to look at it.

Since her divorce from Philip, Lorna's weekend routines had assumed the magical qualities of a ritual—shopping for groceries with Beth on Saturday mornings, laundry on Saturday afternoons (or shopping for the children or sometimes a movie), and anything she could think of to do on Saturday nights to keep herself from letting loneliness creep in like fog from the ocean. On weekends when she had the children, Saturday nights weren't so bad, but on her free weekends they were the pits. They represented both the end of the week, and the beginning of another. Each repetitious week would lead nowhere, would lead to nothing but another weekend spent trying to make Cindy do her homework, or a weekend alone; a weekend in which her major concern was to keep from going crazy with boredom, her life had become so empty.

"Come on, Lorna," Beth said. "You've been staring at that awful blouse for three minutes. It's not your style, and it's not your color, either. Something is definitely bothering you."

"I guess so," Lorna said. She started walking. "I forgot my cents-off coupons again," she said.

"We can pick up circulars at the counter," Beth said. "It's not that important. What's important is that you've got something on your mind you're not talking about."

"Yes, I know," Lorna admitted. "Don't press me, Beth, okay? I don't have it cleared up in my own mind yet. I'll share it with you as soon as I can talk about it coherently."

"Sure. Okay," Beth said. "I won't pressure you. Sometimes it helps to talk, though. Talking's a good way to clear the air."

"I know. But not this time. I'll speak when I can."

"Fine. But remember, I'll give you an ear whenever you need one."

"I know, and thanks. I appreciate it."

They parted in the supermarket, meeting at the meat counter to ask each other's advice, standing in the checkout line together, and arranging for their orders to be delivered. They headed back home. They would have lunch in Beth's apartment, after the rest of the Saturday chores were done. Lorna had spent more money than her budget allowed for, a situation that seemed to be constant. She and Philip had always lived on a tight budget, but these days Lorna was hard pressed to make ends meet.

Lorna and Beth alerted their daughters to wait for the grocery delivery. Then they ran herd on them to make sure they performed the laundry chores and put the groceries away before letting them leave for an afternoon movie. Reluctantly, they took Daniel with them.

By two o'clock, Lorna and Beth were ready for lunch.

"Okay," Beth said. "Chores done. Are you ready yet to tell me the rest of the Len Gold story?"

"There's nothing to tell," Lorna said. She picked up her fork and played with the tuna-fish salad on her plate. "It was just very strange seeing him again, that's all."

"Were you lovers?"

Lorna laughed. "No," she said. "I didn't do anything at all in high school, I practically didn't even pet. Philip was. . . ."

The look on Beth's face made Lorna smile sheepishly.

"Are you trying to tell me that you've never slept with anyone but Philip?" Beth asked.

"I . . . yes," Lorna said.

"I don't believe it!"

"Well, believe it," Lorna said. "It's true. I'm thirty-five plus, and I've never slept with anyone but the man who was my husband, although. . . ."

"Although what?"

"I almost had intercourse with Len once. We actually spent a weekend together, or a night and part of a day. In two motels. It was the most daring thing either of us had ever done."

Beth got up from the table and returned with a bottle of red wine from the refrigerator. "I know I'm not supposed to chill this," she said, "but I like it that way." She uncorked the bottle, poured them both full glasses, and raised hers in salute.

"You want to know what happened, don't you?"

"Well, of course I do, you dope," Beth said.

Lorna got up from the table and took her plate to the sink.

"There you go again," Beth said. "Sometimes I think you wash dishes to avoid things, too."

"I'm not trying to avoid anything," Lorna said. "I'm just trying to sort it out, as I told you earlier."

"Why don't you backtrack a bit, then. Would that help?"

"Okay, I'll try." Lorna looked at the plate in her hands, then firmly placed it on the counter without washing it. She returned to the table. She took a sip of the wine, and then a second. "Both of us had wanted to make love for a long time, but neither of us was ready for that."

"Why? Weren't your friends in high school experimenting with sex?"

"Some of the kids were, I suppose. But I only had a few girl friends, and we were all kept on tight reins. We used to talk about it, but the feelings Len made me feel . . . I've said it before, but I don't know another word for it. They were

37

too intense. I tried to talk about it with my friend Marilen once, and she was frightened, too, but not of the feelings."

"What do you mean?"

"She was dating a college boy for a while, and one weekend he stayed at her place. She lived in an apartment, and he slept on the couch in the living room. In the morning, when she went to the kitchen, he had tossed off the covers. He was still asleep, but she saw his early morning erection. She was afraid of *that*, not her own feelings. At least that's the way it came across to me when she told me the story."

"I had something happen like that once, too," Beth said. "It bothered me, too."

Lorna began to chuckle. An embarrassing memory suddenly surfaced of a night she had necked in a car with a boy she had dated before she met Len. She had let him get on top of her and go through the motions—the first time she had ever allowed such an intimacy. She had been excited and frightened then, too, and the next day the boy told her that he had rubbed the skin of the head of his penis raw against the zipper of his pants.

"Do you realize you're blushing?"

"Am I?" Lorna responded. "Well, why not. I think I must have spent most of my teenage years blushing. Mildred used to compliment me on my nice complexion and the color in my face all of the time. I think it was that I spent a couple of years blushing."

"That's really funny," Beth said.

"Is it? It wasn't so funny then. I wouldn't mind living a lot of the last fifteen years of my life again, but I'd do anything not to have to relive my teens."

"Yes, I know what you mean," Beth said. She finished her wine and poured herself a second glass. "You've barely even taken a taste, Lorna."

Automatically, Lorna reached for her wine, drinking half of it. With an effort, she returned her attention to memories of Len. "Len and I had a lot of classes together, and ate lunch together in the cafeteria nearly every day, but we really didn't start dating for a year even though we were attracted to each other right from the beginning, from the day we met . . . on the first day we entered high school. He wasn't very adept socially—didn't play any sports, didn't go in for many extracurricular activities, didn't have many friends. It's funny. Len wanted to be a writer, but he isn't writing and I married a writer."

"Why didn't you marry him, Lorna?"

"I'm still not sure. What I am sure about is that we should have been lovers, in some kind of an adult sense, but we weren't. I didn't like his attitude about children, and I couldn't picture a future for us. Or maybe it's that the future seemed like a repetition of the way I was already living, and I wanted . . . *something* . . . something *different*." Lorna shrugged. "I certainly have had that. Even so, there were times when Len would kiss me . . . he would kiss me, and. . . ."

"Yes, I know what you mean," Beth said.

Lorna finished her wine and poured herself a second glass. "The first time Len kissed me—sometimes I can still feel how my knees went weak. I mean, he really kissed me, not like the tentative stuff I'd had from the other boys I'd gone out with. And Mildred really liked Len. His father owns a chain of hardware stores in Buffalo. They're quite well off. She was delighted that I'd made what she thought was a very good match. I think she already had visions of Gold grandchildren in her head by that time. That's all she ever really wanted from me, you know. To know that I was safe and comfortably married, and that I would give her grandchildren."

"I can understand why you didn't marry him," Beth said. "You're not the kind of woman who would have been happy in a marriage situation with a man who was ambivalent about having children, but I don't understand why you didn't sleep with him, Lorna. It sounds like he really turned you on."

"Yes, he did. But Mildred—even when I was too young to understand, she began teaching me that sex was wrong unless you were married. She said it a hundred different ways, a hundred different times a week. And that's the only thing she ever told me about sex. She never even explained about menstruation. There wasn't much talk about love, either. Just that whatever it was that happened between men and women was only to happen after marriage. That made for a terrible conflict. My body was sending up one set of signals, and those signals were in conflict with everything I'd been taught."

"Ouch," Beth said. "I got a little bit of that, too, but at least my mother taught me to trust my feelings."

"It shows," Lorna said. "At least you like your mother."

"Yes. Yes, I do," Beth said. "Come on, let's go sit in the living room."

"Okay," Lorna said. She started to take the rest of the dishes into the kitchen.

"No. Leave those. Willemina's coming in at five to do a fast go-through. I've got a date tonight."

"Johnnie Parker?"

"No. A new man. Someone I met at the museum last week. His name is Chuck Landgroff. He's a broker or something."

"I can't keep up with your dating schedule, Beth. There seems to be a new man every week."

"Not really. But I couldn't stand living the way you do, never going out, holing up in the apartment on weekends . . . it would drive me crazy."

"Well, it drives me crazy, but I don't know what to do about it," Lorna said.

"Why don't you go away for a weekend? That would be a step in the right direction."

"Yes. That sounds like a good idea. Maybe I could plan to do that sometime when Philip takes the children."

"That's the right attitude, and I'm going to keep at you to make sure you do it."

Chapter Six

On Sunday, Beth's ex-husband, Bert, came to take Dawn for the day. He included Cindy and Daniel in his plans for a trip to the Museum of Natural History, thus giving Lorna an unexpected day off. She was still feeling confused about both her meeting with Len and the talk she had had with Beth the day before. When Beth suggested that they have brunch together in Greenwich Village, she accepted eagerly, even though the expense would leave her a bit short for the week.

They found an attractive glassed-in sidewalk cafe, took a table by the windows, and ordered one of the special brunches that included Mimosa cocktails, a combination of champagne and orange juice.

"How was your date last night?" Lorna asked.

"So, so," Beth said. "We had a nice dinner and did some dancing, but once we got back to my place he turned into a veritable octopus and I wasn't ready for that."

"How did you get out of it? I had that happen once, and I couldn't think of anything more constructive to do than threaten to call the doorman."

"I told him I was sorry, I found him very attractive, but I was at the tail end of taking a cycle of medication for a very virulent form of vaginitis."

Beth's remark caught Lorna with a mouthful of her Mimosa cocktail, and the look on her face caused Beth to begin to laugh. Soon they were both howling.

"You didn't," Lorna said. "You didn't, did you?"

"Yes, indeed, I did."

On the street outside the cafe, two nice-looking men dressed in the Village uniform of well-pressed blue jeans and jackets stopped momentarily to look at them through the glass window before sauntering on.

"They're probably gay," Beth said. "Even so, you're a different person when you laugh, Lorna. Men look at you. You have an air about you. You look like a woman who knows she's a woman."

"Whatever do you mean by that, Beth?"

"I mean you have your own style. You wear clothes you like because they look well on you, or because they're comfortable, not because they're 'fashionable.' You don't try to look like anyone but you . . . that's all. You're a nice person, and you have values that count."

"You want something, Beth Pilsner," Lorna said. "That's the most outrageous piece of flattery you've tried on me in a long time. I know you, too, you know. So, okay, what's on your mind?"

This time it was Beth's turn to laugh. She pushed aside her drink and ordered a refill when the waiter brought their eggs Benedict and steamed vegetables. She waited until he was out of earshot.

"Okay," she said. "I woke up this morning

thinking about our talk yesterday. You told me a lot about you and Len, but you didn't tell me the most important thing of all."

"Which is?"

"I want to hear about that motel weekend."

"Oh, Lord," Lorna said. "You know, that was over twenty years ago now, and it still bothers me. Looking back, it seems like a comedy of errors, but it didn't seem that way at the time. Parts of it still stand high on my list of all-time embarrassments."

"What happened?"

"Let's see. Where to begin?" Lorna took her time, devoting herself momentarily to her brunch. "Yum," she said, "the hollandaise is delicious!"

"Yes, it is," Beth agreed. "The vegetables are beautiful, too, aren't they?"

"Yes. Thanks. I'm glad you got me out today."

"You're welcome. Now, come on, get on with it."

"Okay. Len and I had been seeing each other for about two years, I guess, although we'd known each other longer than that. We were in our last year of high school. We'd finally gotten to the point where I would . . . where I would touch him every now and then, and sometimes I would let him touch me, although I'd never let him take my clothes off, not even undo my bra."

"God, he must have had the most patience of any man on the face of the earth."

"Yes and no," Lorna said. "He was a virgin, too. The fact is, hindsight tells me that he was as frightened as I was."

"Yes, I can understand that," Beth said.

"Well, this time, finally, he gave me an ultimatum. Either I spent a night with him, or he was going to break things off."

"That was a pretty strong position for him to take."

"Yes, it was. Except here again, hindsight shows that's the only way he could figure out to handle things. Subtlety is something one learns; it certainly isn't part of the average teenager's social repetoire. I wanted loving as much as he did; but he did the asking, and I said yes."

"It took the pressure off, didn't it, having him put things to you like that?"

"Yes. Yes, it did. It was the marrying that was bothering me."

"I understand that."

"So, I told Mildred I was spending a weekend at Marilen's house. I swore Marilen to secrecy and she agreed to cover for me. Len made a reservation for us at a motel a couple of miles outside of Buffalo. He borrowed a car for the weekend. He treated it as if we were going on a honeymoon . . . and that was the first problem."

"What do you mean?"

"Give me a minute, Beth. I want to finish my food here before it gets cold."

"Sure."

When they were done with their meal, the waiter came to remove the dishes and refill their coffee cups. Beth lit a cigarette, and Lorna took one also. She rarely smoked, but enjoyed a cigarette every now and then. She put her elbows on the table, resting her chin on her hands.

"He took me to dinner at a very swanky seafood restaurant . . . candlelight, a pianist playing standards, and he did the ordering: oysters, a bottle of

45

champagne, and lobster. Brandy with our after-dinner coffee."

"Sounds romantic," Beth said.

"It was," Lorna said. "In fact, it was one of the most romantic evenings I've ever had. I was very excited, and scared. I drank too much champagne and I'd never had brandy before. Then we did a little bit of dancing and went to the motel. It was a very cold night—early in February—but even the cold air didn't help very much. The room wasn't any too warm, either. Len was scared, too, but not as scared as I was. And as it turned out, it didn't matter. We walked in the door . . . the room was not very nice . . . cracked beige plaster walls and a flowered quilt that I'll remember all of my life. Even before we took off our coats, Len took me in his arms and began to kiss me. The next thing I knew I was in the bathroom being sick."

"Oh, no!"

"Oh, yes! I don't know which was worse, how bad my body felt or how embarrassed I was. It wasn't just the champagne. It turns out that I can take small amounts of seafood, but I'd never eaten very much of it, and I'm allergic. Hives you wouldn't have believed. Everywhere! Hideous red splotches, itching like crazy."

Beth signaled the waiter for refills of their coffee. "I don't know whether that makes me want to laugh or cry," she said.

"Len was really quite sweet about the whole thing. I didn't throw up for very long. In pretty short order, he helped me out of my dress and put warm towels on me to try to stop the itching from the hives. I wouldn't take off anything else, though. I was absolutely miserable. I spent most of the night crying. We just lay together on the bed and he held me in his arms and tried to keep me from scratching myself raw. Sometime in the middle of the night, the hives went away, and we both fell asleep. I was so embarrassed that I could barely look at him in the morning."

"And then what happened?"

"We checked out of the motel and found a restaurant to have breakfast. We tried to talk, but neither one of us could find any words. We dawdled over coffee, just like we're doing, except that we were dawdling because we didn't know what to do."

"Well, at least he still wanted to spend time with you," Beth said, "even if you didn't make it. I gave my virginity to an unfeeling jerk in a motel room during a college weekend. The next morning he told me to get dressed, drove me to the bus station, and never said another word to me."

"You're kidding!"

"No, I'm not," Beth said. She lit another cigarette, and Lorna took a second one also.

"That must have made you feel like the end of the world," Lorna said.

"It did. But that's another story, and I want to hear the rest of yours."

"Okay. Somehow or other, we got ourselves out of the restaurant, and back into the car. Len was driving. He wasn't heading back into the city, he was just driving, very slowly, taking roads I'm not sure he had ever driven on before. I was still in so much turmoil I didn't even ask him where we were going. There wasn't anywhere I wanted to go, either. I certainly didn't want to go home, and I didn't want to go to Marilen's either. I didn't know what I could say to her. She thought I was spending the weekend at a motel with Len, and I knew she was going to ask me questions I didn't know how to answer."

"Len must have been in the same situation."

"Yes and no. As I said, he really didn't have many friends, and I'm not sure he had told anyone where he was going."

"That seems odd."

"Yes, but that's the way he was then. Well, to make a long story short, about noon, Len unexpectedly pulled the car to the side of the road and stopped. 'I want to try it again, Lorna,' he said. So that's what we did. We found another motel, and we tried it again."

"And what happened?"

"Nothing. Nothing at all. Well, that's not exactly true. This time we undressed, and got into bed. We kissed and touched each other—and Len couldn't get an erection."

Beth grimaced. "Poor both of you," she said.

"Yes," Lorna agreed. "Later in the afternoon, he took me back to Marilen's. I called Mildred and told her I wasn't feeling well and was coming home and that was the end of it."

"What do you mean?"

"I mean just that. I refused to see Len any more after that."

"What!"

"That's right. I stopped seeing him. I was too embarrassed. We had a hard time of it for a while, because we still had time until we graduated from high school, but I didn't date him again after that. I dropped out of chorus, too. He called nearly every day for a few weeks, but I refused to see him."

"That was really cruel, Lorna. I'm surprised."

"Yes. Yes, I suppose it was cruel, but I didn't understand that at the time. It didn't feel cruel. I was too young, and too naive, and too mortified."

"Ouch! Ouch! Ouch!" Beth said. "No wonder that recent meeting upset you."

"Right. And it's even a little worse than that."

"Meaning?"

Lorna shrugged. "I told Philip about Len, after we were married. I told him that Len excited me a lot. When I mentioned the meeting to Philip—"

"You didn't!"

"Yes, I did, although I shouldn't have, and I'm sorry that I did. Because Philip said the strangest thing. He said that sometimes he thinks that Len's presence in our marriage was more of an influence than his affair with Sally Thornton."

"Whatever did he mean by that?"

"I'm not sure," Lorna said. "But. . . ."

"Go on."

"Our sex life. Mine and Philip's. We made love often, but it . . . it wasn't all that terrific for me, Beth. And once . . . oh, Lord, you know, sometimes I *can* be very cruel."

"Everyone, Lorna. Everyone has that in them sometimes, and you have it so much less than practically anyone else I've ever met."

"Really?"

"Really."

"Great," Lorna said. "So all I did once was to tell Philip that he didn't excite me as much as Len used to."

"Yikes," Beth said. "That was really dumb."

"Yes, yes it was," Lorna said. "But you know, it's the truth. I wasn't in love with Len the way I was with Philip. But there was a passion in our relationship, even if it was never consummated, that really was absent in my marriage. Oh, sometimes it was there, but mostly there was a kind of gentleness and. . . ."

"You miss Philip, don't you, Lorna?"

"Yes. Yes, I do. You know, he said something else the other night, too. He asked me if I ever thought we'd made a mistake. And I said yes. Because, sometimes, I do think we made a mistake. Oh damn, that one's Mildred's doing too, you know. I can still hear her talking about fidelity in marriage."

"Would you consider a reconciliation?"

"I don't know, Beth. I don't know. Philip hasn't made any move in that direction, and I'm certainly not about to."

"And what are you going to do about Len?"

"About Len? Why, nothing, of course."

"But don't you know how to get in touch with him?"

"I . . . yes, I know where he works."

"Aren't you curious?"

"I . . . yes. Yes, I am curious. But I told you, he's married, and—"

"I know. I know. 'I won't go out with married men.' Sometimes I think that's your single favorite sentence," Beth said.

"Well, it's true. And. . . ."

"And what?"

"I just can't. I just can't make a move here, don't you understand that? Because I still feel guilty after all these years, and if I called him . . . if I called him, and saw him again, I think I'd . . . I think I'd feel obligated to . . . to see things through now. I'm not a child, and I don't get sick from a couple of glasses of champagne, and I know enough not to overeat shellfish, and Len's an adult, too, and . . . I just can't!"

"He still excites you, doesn't he," Beth said in a moment of understanding. "It excited you, seeing him again."

"Yes," Lorna said. "Yes. And somehow it frightens me even more now than it did then."

Chapter Seven

FRIDAY NIGHT, AFTER PHILIP PICKED UP THE CHILdren, Lorna ate supper alone, read through the previous Sunday's *New York Times Magazine*, which she had not found time for earlier in the week, took a large tumbler of brandy to bed with her, watched an episode of "Dallas," and fell into a troubled sleep. It was the first night she had spent alone in the apartment in nearly a month because of changes in the weekend schedules with Philip, and she was very tired. She was having trouble coming to grips with the disturbing fact that she had expected Len Gold to stop by the store again, had fully expected him to come after her. Yet she was glad that he had not. Beth had often gotten herself involved with married men during the years since her divorce. Lorna had lived through the pain and suffering such situations wrought, and she was determined not to become that masochistic.

But the dreams! The dreams she had been having ever since her meeting with Len! Nearly every night since the meeting she had had trouble sleeping, her memory tormenting her, her body crying out for release. Although she had not always been satisfied, her sex life with Philip had been a full one, even after he had begun his affair with Sally Thornton. Until the day he confessed to her, Lorna had not had an inkling that Philip was finding time to make love to another woman. Nearly every night they had made love or at least had touched and cuddled. The loss of this contact had affected Lorna deeply. She knew it showed on her face, in her posture, in the way she viewed herself and the world around her. It was much more difficult to wake up in the morning, much more difficult to like herself, much more difficult to show affection even toward the children.

What was it Philip had said? "You used to talk about him a lot. . . . Sometimes, I think his presence in our lives was more of an influence on our marriage going sour than my affair with Sally Thornton."

Yes, I did talk about Len a lot, Lorna said to herself, just as she had admitted to Beth. Len was the first man who had ever excited her. The first man who had made her body respond sexually. She had wanted him, had wanted him to make love to her, although she was too young, too naive to understand that what had happened in the motel was no reflection on her.

Oh, curse you, Mildred, curse you for keeping me so innocent! she thought. She instantly regretted it, although Mildred's attitude about sex certainly had contributed to the fact that Lorna and Mildred had never attained the friendship that some mother-daughter relationships reach—a loss Lorna felt deeply. She talked about it often with Beth. Lorna envied Beth's relationship with her mother, just as she was sometimes forced into a jealousy of the alimony and child support payments which Beth received from her ex-husband— enough money to keep her living comfortably without working. If there was a problem in their friendship, it was the conflict between Lorna's difficult reality problems and Beth's cheerful attitude about her easy life. Beth's life seemed to revolve around men, daytime soap operas, occasional visits to art gallerys or museums, movies, and historical novels. Lorna found this difficult to understand.

What was the other thing Philip had said? "Do you ever think we made a mistake, Lorna?"

Yes.

She had thought that often, too, but somehow it was typical that Philip, not she, had been the one to voice it. She had dated a little during the past year. There had been a customer who had come into the store, then he returned a second and third time. There had been a man with whom Beth had fixed her up. A man she had met during her single excursion to a bar one Saturday night when loneliness had settled on her like a physical presence. But that was not her style, and she was usually too tired after a week of work and caring for the children to want to get into a social whirl. In the spring, during her vacation, Philip had taken the children for a week and she had gone to Puerto Rico, but she had met only recently divorced men, all of whom had problems so intense that they literally needed rehabilitation. That wasn't her style, either. She had barely enough energy these days to cope with her own problems, her own life, much less the problems of men with lives shattered like porcelain.

On the following Saturday, after her supermarket trip with Beth, Lorna belatedly called her mother to acknowledge the letter and yearbook which had arrived more than a week before.

"Well," Mildred said. "The mails are certainly taking their time."

"No, Mom," Lorna said. "It's me. I just didn't have the time this past week—"

"Not enough time to make a phone call?"

Lorna shut her eyes and leaned back into the chair, a knot of desperation forming in her gut. What was there about this woman that made her instinctively feel guilty about everything she did?

"Look, Mom, I'm working from nine to six, and there are the kids to take care of—"

"It's all right, Lorna, I understand," Mildred said, although her tone denied the statement.

For a moment, Lorna thought about mentioning the meeting with Len, but she knew it would lead to something that she was not sure she could cope with. Then, to her surprise, Mildred brought up his name.

"I saw Marilen last week, Lorna," Mildred said.

"She mentioned she had seen Len Gold. You know his uncle died a few weeks ago, and he was home for the funeral."

"No, I didn't know that," Lorna said. "How would I know that?"

"He asked about you."

"That's nice."

"Marilen told him you were in New York, working at Willet's."

"Is that what made you send me the yearbook, Mom?" Lorna said, suddenly realizing that the meeting with Len and the arrival of the yearbook might not have been such a coincidence after all. Len had come into Willet's not because of a rude salesgirl, but because he knew she was working there. Yes, Lorna thought. Yes, that's what happened. For some reason she did not understand, she could feel growing anger.

"Lorna? Are you still there?"

"Yes, Mom. Look, I've got to go now. Beth's due in a few minutes," she lied, "and—"

"All right, dear. Give my love to Cindy and Daniel, and next time, please call when they're home so I can talk to them."

"All right."

For a full ten minutes after the call, Lorna sat in the chair by the phone table, staring out the window at the East River. Two tugs were slowly pulling a barge against the current under blue skies studded with scudding cumulus clouds. Across the river, the waterside factories of Brooklyn and Queens were emitting streams of smoke into the air. It was a beautiful fall day—there were even small havens of trees touched with autumn colors. Slowly Lorna began to relax, to rid herself

55

of the tension she felt from her talk with Mildred, although the call had produced less strain than usual. What kind of a fuss would Mildred have made if I'd mentioned Len? she wondered.

She reached for the phone and dialed Beth's number, suddenly anxious to avoid spending the rest of the weekend alone, but Beth was not at home.

On an impulse, Lorna headed for the bedroom. For a moment she stared at the yearbook which was sitting on the dresser where she had put it the week before, then she took it back into the living room. She flipped the pages until she found Len's picture. Unlike her own, which was decidedly unflattering, Len's picture was a good one, capturing the roguish quality he had had even in high school. He had been one of the handsomest boys in the class. Then, unable to stop herself, Lorna flipped the pages until she found the picture of Margot Skillen—now Margot Skillen Gold. Even in the black-and-white picture, one knew she had beautiful auburn hair, that her complexion was perfect. For a long moment, Lorna stared at the picture, then with a sigh she threw the yearbook across the room and a great bittersweet laugh burst from her.

Just as her feelings for Len seemed undiminished by the years since high school, so her dislike of Margot Skillen seemed undimmed. Margot had come "from the wrong side of the tracks." She had had a "reputation." She was an average student who had a penchant for getting into trouble. Once, during a class picnic, she and her boy friend had sneaked off into the woods and hadn't returned by the time the buses to return them to school were ready to leave. The teacher in charge waited for them, after alerting the park ranger. The next day the whole school knew that Margot and her boy friend had been found necking on a patch of moss near a little creek.

It wasn't that that had bothered Lorna, though. In fact, she thought the episode was very daring on Margot's part. What bothered her was an encounter they had had in the chorus changing room one afternoon toward the end of the first year that Lorna and Len had been dating.

"I like Len a lot, you know," Margot had said.

"So do I."

"Well, I'm just warning you. When and if the two of you break up, I'm going after him."

None of the girls whom Lorna had been friends with at that time would have even considered making such a remark and, although Lorna had never told Len about the brief but blunt exchange of words, she had let him know that she didn't like Margot.

That little exchange had happened a lifetime before, and yet it still seemed as vivid as the day it occurred. The thought that another woman might try to take Len away from her had frightened Lorna as much as her own feelings had.

Maybe—just maybe—Philip was right. How was it possible for feelings remaining so strong after twenty years not to have affected their marriage?

Yes, Lorna admitted to herself.

Yes. It was possible.

And it was impossible, too, because there was nothing she could do about it!

Chapter Eight

ON THE SECOND FRIDAY OF EVERY MONTH, LORNA
spent the day at Willet's checking stock, writing up
order forms, and working with the bookkeeper.
Despite the usual increase in sales associated with
the back-to-school September phenomenon, the
figures for the previous quarter were lower than
the year before. She estimated that the usual
October slump was worse this year also. Most of
the difficulty was competition in the form of a
discount stationery supply house which had
opened a block away during the summer. The new
store had not affected sales to Willet's steady
business customers, but it had severely lowered
the number of off-the-street buyers who came in.
There was nothing Lorna could do about it. On
this Friday, Bob Pertkin, the bookkeeper, a serious young man, passed along word that, if sales
did not pick up by the beginning of the next
month, she would have to dismiss one of her
part-time salespeople. And that, of course, meant
having to let Gail go.

The news seemed appropriate. During the
night, the first cold spell of the year had moved
into the metropolitan New York area, accompanied by gray skies. Thanksgiving was still two
weeks away, but already it felt like winter. A

childhood spent in the savage winters in upstate Buffalo had not helped Lorna to learn to enjoy the pleasures of the winter. Mildred had always been an overprotective mother, and Lorna had never learned to ski or enjoy other outdoor sports associated with snow. The onset of winter weather usually brought depression to her, although, thanks to Philip, Cindy and Daniel had not inherited her dislike of cold. Lorna had accompanied them on numerous skiing weekends when there was money to do so, although she herself had never participated, preferring to spend her time reading or sitting by the fire in the lodge.

During the past year, since the divorce, because money had been very tight, there had been only one weekend when Philip had taken Cindy and Daniel skiing, a situation about which the children had complained bitterly.

Lorna sighed to herself.

Perhaps Len was right, and this time there would be substantial money from Philip's new book. Not that it would do her much good.

"Well, Lorna, here's the situation," Bob Pertkin said, showing her the tally sheet for October. It was worse than Lorna had thought it was going to be. "Mr. Willet isn't going to be very happy."

"I know," Lorna said. "I've been thinking it might be worthwhile trying a line of leather goods . . . briefcases, attaches, wallets. We're still drawing customers for expensive items . . . pens, for instance."

"I don't know," Bob said. "Maybe."

"And good leather desk diaries. Even our business customers ask for those sometimes."

"Well, that's certainly a good idea. Do you want to mention it to Mr. Willet or shall I?"

"Go ahead, Bob. You do it," Lorna said. "You'll be seeing him this afternoon, won't you?"

"Yes. He's not going to want to see them, but I've got to show him the figures."

"Okay. And here." She took a card from the desk drawer. "A salesman was in last week with attractive samples. I think we could do well carrying his line. They have a favorable discount and return policy."

"All right, Lorna. I'll see what I can do."

"Good. At least that way maybe I can talk him into letting me have another month or two before I have to fire Gail. It really would leave me with more work than I can handle comfortably."

"I know," Bob said, "but the figures—"

"The figures are inhuman," Lorna said. "If something doesn't happen I'm going to have to fire a widow who can barely make ends meet just a few weeks before Christmas."

"I don't think Mr. Willet will make you do that, Lorna. I'm sure he won't leave you shorthanded for the Christmas rush."

"Well, I hope not."

Bob packed the papers away in his briefcase and shrugged into his jacket. "The cold caught me by surprise this morning."

"I think a lot of people were caught unprepared," Lorna said. She stood up from the desk in the stockroom. "I'll walk you to the door."

"Okay. I'll give you a call later to let you know how Mr. Willet responds if he doesn't want to call. Otherwise, I'll see you next month."

"Okay. Fine."

Lorna opened the door to the main part of the store and stopped.

Len was standing by the cash register, talking to Gail, who nodded in her direction.

Len turned to look at her. He was wearing a well-cut Burberry raincoat with the collar turned up, and he had had a haircut. This time he wasn't wearing his glasses, and, even at a distance, Lorna could see the intense feeling in his eyes.

It had been nearly a month since their first encounter. During the past week, Lorna had finally begun to break free of the torment the other meeting had caused. Now she could feel her legs go weak and the color rush to her face.

"Lorna? Are you all right?"

"I'm fine," Lorna said, getting a grip on herself. She stood aside and gave Bob room to come through the door. She walked with him to the main entrance of the store, ignoring Len although she could feel the steady gaze of his eyes upon her. If it had not been so cold, she might very well have simply walked out of the store with Bob and just kept going, anywhere, anywhere at all to avoid having to turn and look into the depths of Len's eyes, the green eyes that locked with hers the minute Bob had left the store and the door closed behind him.

"Hi, Lorna," he said.

"Hello, Len."

"Excuse me, Lorna," Gail said. "I need a new tape for the register. I'm going back into the stockroom for a minute."

"I . . . all right," Lorna said, although she knew Gail had replaced the tape in the register only that morning.

Did it show that much? Lorna wondered. She looked down at her hands. It was weeks since she had found time to give herself a manicure, and she had the sudden horrible desire to ball her hands up into fists and hide them behind her back.

"That was nice of her," Len said, nodding toward Gail who was nearly at the stockroom door.

"Yes. Yes, I suppose it was," Lorna agreed.

Len reached out and took Lorna's hand. "Don't be upset," he said.

"I'm not upset," Lorna lied.

"Yes, you are. I . . . look, that wasn't very nice of me, that last remark of mine on the library steps."

"Don't worry about it, Len. It didn't mean anything."

"Yes. It did. It was flip, and it wasn't what I wanted to say at all."

"What did you want to say?"

"I wanted to say . . . I wanted to say I still have strong feelings for you, Lorna. And I think you still have some feeling for me. Don't you think we could see a bit of each other and—"

"No. I don't," Lorna said, pulling away and heading for safety behind the cash register counter. "Go away, Len. Please. This isn't going to do either of us any good."

"I'm not going away, Lorna. If it isn't today, it will be next week, but sometime you'll unbend. Please. At least have dinner with me some night. Let me—"

"No."

"Yes," he said. There was a decisiveness in his voice which Lorna knew she would be unable to resist. "I haven't been able to get you out of my thoughts, Lorna, not since the day I came here last month."

"You knew I was working here. You knew you would find me here," Lorna said. "It wasn't an accident." She opened the cash register and unrolled some pennies even though there was an ample supply in the drawer.

"I . . . yes," Len said. "Marilen mentioned it to me."

Lorna glanced at him quickly, then looked down at the cash register again, pushing the drawer closed. "I know. Mildred told me. She saw Marilen a few days after your uncle's funeral. I'm sorry about your loss. You didn't mention it."

"No, I didn't. If I had, you would have known. It was silly of me to lie, but I thought it would be easier."

"Why did you come looking for me? Why did you want to stir things up?"

"I'm not sure," Len said honestly. "Still, I'm not sorry, and I wish you weren't either. I'm not asking you to do anything but spend a little time with me, that's all. It's not as if I'm asking you to run away to Tahiti with me, for heaven's sake!"

And suddenly Lorna laughed. "Right," she said. "Right you are."

"Will you then?"

"Will I what?"

"Have dinner with me? Tonight?"

"No. I can't," Lorna said. "Not tonight." Philip was coming to pick up Cindy and Daniel, and Lorna knew she dared not accept the invitation without the protection of the children at home waiting for her return.

"All right. Then how about next Tuesday?"

"I . . . all right," Lorna said. "But let's make it early, okay? I'm done here about six, and I'll have to be home by eight or eight-thirty at the latest to make sure the children are settled in and have their homework under control."

"You don't have to explain," Len said. "Next Tuesday it is."

"And Len."

"Yes?"

"No lobster, okay?"

Len laughed. "Okay," he said. "It's a deal."

That afternoon Bob Pertkin called to let Lorna know that Mr. Willet had agreed to let her try the new line of leather goods on a three-month consignment basis, but he also gave her the bad news that she was indeed going to have to let Gail go. She could keep her on until the end of the year, but was going to have to do without her after that even if sales increased substantially during Christmas. The timing of the announcement to Gail was left up to her. Lorna decided to wait for a few weeks, feeling terrible about it but ruthlessly self-protective. If she told Gail now, she might leave and try to find another job before Christmas, leaving Lorna seriously shorthanded during the busy few weeks before the end of the year.

"I hate myself for it, Beth," Lorna said that Saturday, "but I just can't risk her leaving before then. It's lousy, isn't it?"

"Yes, it is," Beth said. "But maybe I can help. I'll ask Bert if his personnel department can find a job for her." Bert, Beth's ex-husband, owned a chain of nearly twenty gift shops scattered throughout Manhattan and the boroughs of Queens and Brooklyn. "They're always looking for people."

"Would you, Beth? I'd really appreciate it," Lorna said.

"Sure. Where does she live?"

"Gail? I think she lives in Queens," Lorna said.

"Okay." And in an uncharacteristic move, Beth immediately went to the telephone and called Bert, explaining the situation to him. "Well," she said when she hung up the receiver, "he'll do what he can. Meaning he'll have them keep the first opening in January available for her."

"Terrific!" Lorna said.

"Now, what about you? It's been weeks since I suggested that you go away for a weekend, and here you are, still without plans."

Lorna shrugged. "Christmas is coming up next month, and if I go away I won't have money to buy presents for Daniel and Cindy. Besides. . . ."

"Besides what?"

"Len. He came back last week. I'm . . . I'm having dinner with him next week."

"Well, good for you," Beth said. "That ought to do you good."

"Maybe," Lorna said. "And, then again, maybe not."

Still, Lorna spent time on herself over the weekend, giving herself the long-overdo manicure, conditioning her hair, soaking in the tub with bath oil, all the time chiding herself for being a silly goose. But, hard as she tried, it was impossible for her to convince herself that there was nothing more in the upcoming evening than a simple dinner date with an old friend. She was playing with fire, she knew she was playing with fire, but, somehow, by the time Philip returned the children on Sunday night she had convinced herself that she could handle it.

"Hi, Mom," Cindy said, coming to give Lorna a hug.

"Hi, Cindy-Bear. I missed you."

"I was only gone for a few days."

"Well, I missed you anyway," Lorna said.

"Hey, you smell good."

Lorna shrugged. "I soaked in the tub with some bath oil this afternoon."

"Your hair looks nice, too," Philip said.

"Why, thank you, Philip."

Philip put Cindy's overnight bag down in the hallway.

"How about a cup of coffee?" he asked. "There's something the matter with the heater in the car, and I'm cold."

"Sure. Do you want hot chocolate, kids?"

"Yup," Daniel said. "And you should see what Mr. Ditman got. The strangest dog. What is he again, Dad?"

"A borzoi."

"That's a funny choice for Ben," Lorna said. "I would have thought he would have liked a spaniel or a setter."

"I agree," Philip said. "Still, it's a nice dog."

"How about letting us get a dog?" Daniel asked.

"Not a chance," Lorna said. "And what about homework?"

"I did mine," Daniel said.

"Cindy?"

"Well, I've got a little," she said, "but I'll do it

66

later." Cindy headed for the den, and immediately there was the sound of the television set clicking on.

"Put on the water, would you, Philip?" Lorna headed after her daughter. "And just what is a 'little?'" she asked Cindy.

"I've got a current events page to do for social studies, and a bit of reading for English."

"How much is 'a bit?'"

"Well, I have a report due on Wednesday."

"What kind of a report?"

"A book report. But it's okay. I'm just going to be late with it, that's all."

"What do you mean, you're going to be late?"

"I haven't picked my book out yet."

"You haven't. . . ." Lorna could feel a red anger rising in her. Cindy's cavalier attitude about school was impossible for her to understand. Recently she had taken to lying by omission when Lorna asked her about upcoming assignments.

"I lost my library card, and I knew if I asked you for extra money you were going to say no. But I got my new card on Friday, and I'll get the book tomorrow. Honest."

Lorna reached over and flicked off the television set. "Look, Cindy—"

"Hey, don't Mom. I've got to watch the news for current events," Cindy said.

"I thought you were supposed to get your information from the newspaper."

"We have a choice, and it's easier from the television."

For a long moment Lorna stood looking at her daughter lounging on the sofa, then she left the room before she did or said something she would

67

be sorry about. Philip was in the kitchen, pouring water over the coffee grounds. Lorna got the milk from the refrigerator and began to make the hot chocolate.

"We've got to do something about Cindy," she said. "She's really in trouble in school. She's not doing her homework, and she's letting everything go until the last minute. I don't know what to do."

"I don't either," Philip said. "She was doing just fine in school until last year."

Until our divorce, you mean, Lorna thought, although she did not say the words. But it was true. The separation and divorce had affected Cindy much more than it had Daniel, who had always been the more resilient of the children. And along with the unspoken words was the unspoken resentment on Philip's part because it had been Lorna, not Philip, who had insisted on the divorce.

"Ben sends his regards," Philip said. "We had a pleasant weekend. He had some good news, too. *Clear Lake* has hit the 'A' list at Book-of-the-Month Club."

"What does that mean?" Lorna asked.

"It means it's being considered seriously as a selection for late spring or early summer," Philip said. "If that happens, there's an odd kind of a feedback that affects the hardcover sales. The book will almost certainly hit the best-seller lists, not to mention a very handsome dollar guarantee from the book club."

"Well, that is good news," Lorna said. "You've worked very hard to try to make a decent living as a writer. It would be good if that happened."

And it would have been even better if it had happened earlier, Lorna thought, hating herself for being unable to control her momentary jealousy although she realized that it was impossible for her to feel otherwise. Part of Philip's impending success was due to her, to the years she had supported him in her role as wife, but none of the success would be hers. It was exactly the recognition of this that had prompted her to find the job at Willet's in the first place. The irony was that the job had gotten her out of the house, had given Philip time he didn't want or need, time which he filled by beginning his affair with Sally Thornton. . . .

"Has he stopped by again?" Philip asked unexpectedly.

"Who?" Lorna said, although she knew full well Philip was referring to Len.

"Marsh—Len Gold."

"No," Lorna lied, although she did not know why.

"I'm surprised."

"Why?"

"I don't know," Philip said. "I thought you two would begin to see each other. I mentioned it to Ben over the weekend, and he thought the whole thing was a splendid coincidence also, the kind of thing I could never get away with in one of my novels."

"Well, as it turns out, it probably wasn't such a coincidence," Lorna said. "I spoke to Mildred over the weekend. Len was in Buffalo a while back for an uncle's funeral and he spent some time with Marilen. He asked about me, and she told him where I was working. Marilen mentioned it to Mildred; that's what prompted Mildred to send me the yearbook."

"Oh," Philip said. "Well that explains it, then."

"Yes." Lorna gave the hot chocolate to Daniel and Cindy. A half hour later Philip took his leave. There was something about their conversation which bothered her, a strain between them that seemed different. She did not let herself dwell on it, but she suspected that her own attitude was responsible. She had spent a great deal of time over the weekend getting ready for her Tuesday night date with Len, and it had made the hours pass quickly. She had not experienced her usual weekend depression. Monday morning she was up and out of bed feeling excited about the week to come even though Thanksgiving was on Thursday and she would be spending the holiday alone for the first time in her life.

Somehow, having made the decision to have dinner with Len had pushed her through a barrier. She was no longer afraid but was looking forward to their meeting—looking forward to it with pleasurable anticipation.

Chapter Nine

THE FIRST THING MONDAY MORNING, BECAUSE OF Beth's promise of help from Bert to find Gail a job, Lorna broke the news to her that she was soon to be let go from Willet's. There was really no certainty that a position would be found in one of Bert's stores, or that the transition would be easy, still, Gail was grateful for the help Lorna offered to get her settled in a new position, and the task proved to be less difficult than Lorna had thought it would be. Further, much to Lorna's relief, Gail promised to see things through the Christmas season so, at least, that problem was solved with relative ease.

The matter of Cindy's report card, which Lorna found waiting for her when she arrived home from work was a different matter. Cindy had failed two subjects, and had a barely passing grade in a third.

"I suppose they give us our report cards now to take the edge off, to let us have Thanksgiving week to get back into your good graces," Cindy said, offering neither explanations nor apologies for her dismal grades.

The report card was so bad, in fact, that Lorna could do little more than shrug, although anger and disappointment were swirling around inside her desperately seeking escape. Somehow, the thought of the following evening helped keep Lorna from screaming at Cindy, which she knew would do no good. She did find herself picking at both of her children for small things during the remainder of the evening. She was in a strange mood, one she could not categorize—she wasn't sure she liked it, although she realized that it was a buffer right now between her and her daughter, and for that she was grateful.

On Tuesday morning, Lorna dressed with unusual care, from the skin out. The shock of Cindy's report card had not really dimmed during the night, but it was still not strong enough to keep a sense of delicious anticipation from bubbling up within her.

"Hey! Bacon!" Cindy said at the breakfast table. "I thought you were really angry with me, Mom."

"I am," Lorna said, "but that doesn't mean I can't give you a good breakfast this morning."

"Now, don't go feeling guilty, Mom," Daniel said.

"What do you mean?"

"It's that article in the magazine you left in the bathroom," Daniel said. "The one about protein being a good way to start the day. I bet you think you haven't been taking good enough care of us, and that's why Cindy's not doing well in school."

"God, Danny," Cindy said, "sometimes you sound like an old man."

"Why? Just because I read more than you do?"

"That isn't everything," Cindy said. "There's more to life that just books, you know."

"What? Hanging around with friends? Like you do with Dawn all the time?"

72

"It wouldn't do you any harm to be a little bit more social," Cindy said.

"Come on, you two, stop it this instant," Lorna said. "I woke up feeling okay this morning and I don't want to have you squabble away my good mood."

"What's going on?" Cindy asked.

"Well," Lorna said, "if you must know, I have a dinner date this evening."

"Date!" Cindy said. "Does that mean you won't be home when we get home from school?"

"I'm never home when you get home from school."

"You know what I mean," Cindy said. "I mean after work."

"No. You'll have to fend for yourselves tonight. I've left some chopped meat in the refrigerator. You can make hamburgers or a meatloaf."

"Oh, darn," Cindy said. "I don't feel like—"

"Don't, Cindy," Lorna said. "I'm upset enough with you without having an argument about this."

"Who are you going out with?"

"An old friend. Someone I knew when I was growing up in Buffalo. His name is Len. Len Gold."

"Len Gold," Cindy said. "I've heard you talk about him. He was your boy friend in high school."

"Yes, that's right."

"How come you're going out with him?" Cindy asked.

"He stopped by the store a while back and he asked me out for dinner tonight; that's all."

"What time will you be home?" Daniel asked.

"I'll be home by eight-thirty or nine at the

latest. And you, young lady," Lorna said to Cindy, "I'll expect you to have all of your homework done. You know I'm going to have to tell your father about the report card."

Cindy pushed her eggs around on her plate. Then she said, "I know that, but. . . ."

"But what?"

"Part of it isn't my fault," Cindy said. "I really didn't understand the instructions our English teacher gave us. I really didn't know that she wanted us to hand in our journal entries every week. Look, I won't make any excuse at all where science is concerned, I just don't understand it enough even to ask questions. I'm way in the back of the room and there are forty kids in the class. But what happened in English . . . that's something else again. I tried to hand in the assignments. I thought we had to hand them in just once a month like I did last year."

"Did you talk to your teacher? What did she say?"

"She wouldn't listen to me, Mom. Honest. Next week, during Open School Week, would you talk to her? I did all the assignments and I tried to hand them in and she would not accept them."

There was a look of naked pleading on Cindy's face and Lorna realized that she believed her daughter. Still, to have failed two subjects and to have gotten a barely passing mark in a third was so extraordinary that she did not know how to cope with the situation. And what was Philip going to say? There was no way she could keep the news from him. He was going to blame it on her, of course, say that she was not doing a proper job as a mother—and yet, some part of her refused to dwell on the problem.

A year—it had been at least a year since Lorna had woken up in the morning with a sense of anticipation for the day ahead, and she wasn't going to let anything—not anything—affect her mood, not even the reality that her daughter was in serious trouble at school.

"Finish up, the both of you," she said. "Hurry up, now. It's nearly time for you to leave and I have to get to work also."

"Okay, Mom. Sure," Daniel said.

He finished the last mouthful of his breakfast and took his plate to the sink. Cindy, on the other hand, finished her breakfast and left her plate on the table. It was only with prodding that Lorna got her to perform any simple early morning chore. As she had done a million times during the past year, Lorna shook her head in desperation, wondering how Cindy would ever make a go of things in life. She seemed to expect that things would be done for her. That somehow, mysteriously, food would always appear on the table and laundry would always be done—that problems as difficult as the ones she was having with her English teacher at school would be solved by some external circumstance. They were so different, her children, Daniel so much less rebellious. And then the children were in their coats and there were good-bye kisses at the door.

Although she would not have admitted it for the world, Lorna actually enjoyed the fifteen minutes it took to clean up the kitchen after breakfast. It was a small slice of solitude in the comfortable surroundings of her home before her day at Willet's. This morning she rushed through the dishes to give herself a few extra minutes in front of the mirror checking her appearance before donning her coat and heading for work.

Now that the weather had gotten colder, Lorna took a bus uptown to work if it looked as if there would not be a long wait. When the weather was nice, she generally walked to work, savoring the exercise and carefully putting aside the bus fare she saved to cover the cost of dry cleaning the soft wool sweaters she loved to wear in the winter. She refused to give them up, although it was certainly less expensive and easier to take care of synthetic-blend clothing.

Tuesday and Thursday afternoons were generally slow at Willet's and Lorna worked the store with only one salesperson in addition to herself. By the time she had checked the daily sales slips, Len was waiting for her.

As he had the first time he had come into the store, he carried his beautiful saddle-soaped leather briefcase. He helped Lorna into her coat, waited while she closed the metal shutters and locked up the store for the night, then hooked her arm through his.

"I took a chance," he said. "I hope you like Japanese food."

"Yes," Lorna said. "I haven't had it too often, but I enjoy it when I do."

"Fine," Len said. "Because I made reservations for us not too far from here."

Soon they were settled in a tatami compartment in a handsome restaurant on Forty-sixth Street. With Lorna's approval, Len ordered a meal of sushi, teriyaki, grilled and glazed vegetables, and saki to drink.

"See?" Len asked. "Easy, right? Not that it's exactly like old times. Still, it feels very natural for us to be sharing food together, doesn't it?" He poured them both small cups of the warmed saki that the kimono- and obi-clad waitress brought with bowls of clear miso soup.

"Yes, I suppose so," Lorna said, "although I doubt if there was one Japanese restaurant in all of Buffalo twenty years ago."

"No, I don't suppose there was," Len said, "And if anyone had told me that I would develop a taste for raw fish I would have thought they were loony."

"It took me a long time to learn to like it, too, although I don't think I'll ever really crave octopus or squid."

"Are we going to talk about sea creatures all night?" Len said.

"No." And we're not going to talk about my daughter's report card, either, Lorna told herself firmly. She took a small sip of her saki. It was warm, and left a pleasant cleansing taste in her mouth, a delicious contrast to the nourishing well-seasoned soup. She could feel herself relaxing.

"Why don't you tell me what made you decide to look me up now?" she asked. "I'm sure you thought about it before this. I'll admit the thought crossed my mind also, although I'm not a very adventurous woman. I never would have tried to find you, but I suppose it is possible that if Philip and I—"

"Yes. If you and Philip had stayed married,

CAROL STURM SMITH

eventually we would have met at one of his Brockton publication parties. I suppose the real coincidence is that we *didn't* meet because of that connection." Len laughed. "You know, about six or seven years ago, on one of my rare trips to Buffalo, I bumped into Marilen, just like I did this time when I went home for my uncle's funeral. She told me you were married to a writer, but she couldn't remember his name."

"Yes, I can see that that is amusing in retrospect," Lorna said.

"It's funnier than that," Len said. "After Marilen gave me that piece of information, I had a fantasy that your husband *was* a Brockton author, and that we'd meet some day at a party. Your husband would get drunk . . . I've seen that happen a few times . . . and I'd come to the rescue and spirit you away for a weekend somewhere. In the fantasy, you were reluctant, like a heroine in an historical romance, although I overcame your resistance with my roguish charm, good looks, and sexy nature."

Lorna did not even attempt to stifle her laugh, a laugh which seemed to dissipate whatever tension there was still between them. The waitress, who brought their sushi at that moment, graced them both with a smile acknowledging her pleasure at their pleasure.

"Surprisingly, though," Len continued, "when I'd think about you in any situation, I was pretty sure that if we ever did meet again you would be just as glad to see me as I would be to see you. I was sure you thought about me sometimes."

"Pretty egotistical!" Lorna said.

"No, not at all," Len said. "We spent a great

78

deal of time together, Lorna. One just doesn't forget friends like that. Oh, maybe you do if they were people you knew in grade school, but not when you shared the kind of intensity we shared. I thought about you; ergo, you thought about me. Neither one of us are the kind of people to invest time in completely one-sided relationships."

Lorna stopped herself from making a snap reply to this flat statement of Len's, and busied herself with unwrapping the cellophane-packaged chopsticks and selecting her first piece of sushi. There was something about the way Len had spoken for her as well as for himself that bothered her, although he had often done that when they were . . . what? Courting? Keeping company? Exploring what it was to be a teenager? Even now, there was no word or phrase Lorna could call to mind that adequately described what had been between them. Perhaps simple friendship came closest, a friendship which had included feelings of desire and passion for each other.

Len was also quiet for a long time, then he helped himself to the first piece of his sushi, finished his saki, poured himself another cup and offered a refill to Lorna. She shook her head. Len downed that glass also and poured out the remainder into his small blue-and-white porcelain cup. He signaled the waitress to bring a second carafe. They small-talked a bit while finishing their first course, which had been beautifully prepared and was delicious. Before she was finished, Lorna did allow Len to refill her cup. The food she was eating would take the edge off, although she knew saki was powerful.

"People talk a lot about the changes a woman

goes through when she approaches forty," Len said then. "But men go through changes, too, and, in some ways, it's just as difficult. I'm set with Brockton, you know, but even so it's something I think about."

"What do you mean?"

"As far as a job goes, it's not bad, not bad at all. But Brockton's a family business and, no matter how well I'm doing, I'm still only doing as well as an employee can do."

"I'm still not sure I know what you mean," Lorna said.

"It's a closed company. All the stock privately held. There was a time . . . I had dreams, Lorna, and I've made a lot of compromises in my life I never thought I would when I was a kid."

"What kind of compromises?"

Len shrugged. "The kind of compromises all men make who find themselves married and parents before they're old enough to realize what a serious commitment and responsibility they have taken on."

"Yes," Lorna said. "I don't understand the details of your particular situation, but I know what you're saying."

"So, I'm set. But it also means I've had to come to terms with the knowledge that I'm never really going to be my own person, that to some extent I've *never* been my own person. I work for my family; I don't really work for myself . . . not for that part of myself that's an individual and not a husband or a father. My time is never my own. Oh, that's not really true; I can vary my schedule a bit if I have to or want to; but, well, it's not like being a writer."

"Ah," Lorna said, "so that's it."

"No," Len said hastily, reaching out and taking Lorna's hand. "Don't get me wrong. That wasn't a snide dig at Philip. Or jealousy, either. I gave up my ambitions in that direction a long time ago. I've been in the business long enough to know how difficult things are for writers, for all creative people who have to be self-starters all the time. I'm not wishing for a trade of occupations, that wasn't what I meant at all. But sometimes, sometimes. . . ."

"Go on, Len." The feel of Len's hand on hers was as warming as the saki; it pleased her, and she made no move to disengage herself from the intimacy. It was Len who broke the contact, and when he did so Lorna was sorry.

"I had a chance once, a while back, to get a small publishing business started with a friend, and I didn't have the guts to do it. It frightened me too much. It would have taken every penny I had and every penny I could have borrowed. I just didn't have it in me to take the plunge."

"What did Margot think about it?"

"Margot? She didn't encourage me. She was afraid, too. We have three sons to provide for, to put through college. Brockton is very good to their employees. There's scholarship money available." Again, Len reached for his saki cup; again, Lorna allowed him to refill her cup. The remainder of their excellent meal was brought and served. The beef teriyaki was juicy and tender, perfectly cooked; the vegetables retained their crispness, the natural flavors enhanced by the skillful way they had been cut for serving and the glaze which added color and flavor.

"Have you ever thought . . . do you think it would have been different if Margot *had* encouraged you?"

"Maybe," Len said. Then he looked Lorna full in the face, a smile causing his dimples to appear although it was a smile touched with sadness. "No, no *maybes,*" he said. "It *would* have made a difference. I would have done it, although there's no telling what would have happened. Publishing isn't a business where you can second-guess all that easily, but at least I would have given it a shot. Instead, I stayed where I was, and put the extra energy which thinking about the deal gave me into my work at Brockton. It paid off. I got my promotion. But as I said, I'm working for them, and I guess I always will."

"You're not really all that sorry, are you?"

"I'm not sure," Len said. "One thing it did do, however, was to make me look you up when Marilen told me where you were working."

"Why?" Lorna said. "I don't see the connection."

Len shrugged. "Up until this point, you were the only other piece of unfinished business in my life that might have made a real difference in how I perceive myself, my accomplishments."

"I suppose you mean that as a compliment," Lorna said. "Or at least, I'll take it as one."

"Yes," Len said. "I don't mean to imply that I'm sorry I married Margot. She's a good wife, a good mother, and our boys are children I'm proud of. But you, Lorna. You were my first choice, and nothing, not even time, can change that."

Len's eyes were burning into her with the

intensity of a magnifying glass reflecting sunrays. Lorna looked away from him, unable to tolerate the glimpse of his inner feelings which he offered. From the main dining room came the incongruous sound of a tray of dishes being dropped, something one expected anywhere but here in this intimate alcove. The sound underlined the moment, and both Len and Lorna reacted with amusement.

Len shook his head and glanced at his watch. He signaled for the waitress. "It's nearly nine," he said. "If I don't get you home, you won't come out with me again."

"I had no idea!" Lorna said.

"You know what they say about time passing fast when one's having fun."

On an impulse, Lorna held her hand out to Len. "Yes," she said. "Yes. The food was delicious, and thank you for being so open about your feelings with me. I've had a good time. I'm glad I accepted your invitation."

"Will you accept another?"

"Maybe," Lorna said.

Len took Lorna's hand, squeezed it gently, but released it almost immediately. "Since the best you can offer is indecision," he said, "I'm going to make you wait. Sometime or other I'll stop by, or call you at the store."

"All right. That would be fine."

"Do you have plans for Thursday?"

"Sure, everyone has plans for Thanksgiving," Lorna said, although, in fact, she didn't have. Len's mention of the holiday decidedly altered her lighthearted mood. The children were going with

Philip to his married brother's house on Thursday, so she knew she had a difficult and lonely day ahead of her.

"Good. I wish you a happy turkey, and all the trimmings."

"Thanks, and the same to you and yours."

Len paid the waitress, retrieved their coats from the cloakroom, and flagged a taxi which was cruising outside the restaurant. He held the door for Lorna, and gave her address to the driver.

Lorna looked at him curiously.

"I checked you out at the office," he said. "I wanted to know where you lived."

He closed the cab door behind her, making a motion for her to roll down the window, which she did. He bent and kissed her lightly on the lips. "I won't keep you waiting too long," he said.

"Good," Lorna said. She closed the window, waved, and the cab drove off.

Lorna settled back against the seat.

Good, she thought to herself.

Good.

Chapter Ten

Even THE YEAR BEFORE, WHEN SHE HAD CINDY and Daniel with her, Thanksgiving was more difficult for Lorna than the Christmas and New Year holidays. During the long Christmas vacations, while they were still married, Lorna and Philip had taken the children to her mother's home in Buffalo every other year. This meant skiing for Philip, Cindy, and Daniel and a break in the domestic routine for Lorna because Mildred was intensely jealous of her kitchen and did not really even like help with the dishes. Alternatively, they had gone to Philip's parents' winter place in Florida, which Lorna infinitely preferred.

But Thanksgivings had always been joyous affairs over which Lorna and Philip had presided. She had spent days in preparation, cooking wonderful feasts for Philip's family, who had joined them each of the previous ten years except for the last. Lorna missed the cooking and fussing, and the boisterous good company of the Robinsons. Philip's father had stayed in touch with Lorna, as had his brother, Howard, and sister, Norma, who was unabashedly single and took her position as aunt to both Philip's and Howard's children with cheerful seriousness. But Ann, Philip's mother, whom Lorna loved and respected—more than she loved and respected her own mother, she sometimes thought—had been incensed by the divorce, and had not spoken to Lorna in more than a year.

Before she made the final decision to insist upon a separation prior to the divorce, Lorna had many long talks with Ann Robinson. She told her the truth about Philip's affair with Sally Thornton.

"You're crazy, Lorna," Ann said. "There's no excuse for Philip to be acting the way he's acting . . . it's dumb of him to have an affair, and with someone living in the same building, no less! Still, you know as well as I do that it's just a fling. He's not in love with the woman. There is no reason to break up your marriage because of this. Oh, of course, it will be hard for you to trust him again for a while, but really, Lorna—a little bit of outside sex is highly overrated as a means of judging whether or not a marriage is successful."

What would have happened if she had listened to Ann instead of Mildred, Lorna wondered. No doubt, she would still be married. No doubt, she and Philip would have worked the whole thing out. But isn't it always easier with hindsight? she thought.

And would Thanksgivings always be this awful?

"I . . . look, Lorna, you know you'd be welcome if you wanted to come with us, right now, on the spur of the moment," Philip said when he came to pick up the children early Thanksgiving Day. "There are a few situations where we could at least try to be a bit more flexible. You insisted on keeping the children last year, even though they were invited to my brother's, just like this year."

"Don't, Philip, please," Lorna said. "If it were just. . . ."

"Just what?"

"Just Howard and Miriam . . . but Ann. She hasn't spoken to me for a year."

"Well, maybe it's time to see if you two can change that," Philip said. "Cindy and Daniel are still her grandchildren, no matter what, and you're still their mother. The divorce doesn't change that, and Ann knows it. It's just that . . . well, she's as stubborn as you are."

"Thanks, Philip, but no thanks. I'm not ready to take the initiative here, but I'd appreciate it if you'd give my love to folks."

"Sure. I'll do that."

Even with as firm a denial of his invitation as that, Philip hesitated at the door of the apartment, and Lorna knew he was still hoping that she would change her mind. During the previous weekend, thinking ahead to Tuesday's dinner with Len had kept her from dwelling on thoughts of Thanksgiving coming up. Before that, she had considered changing her mind and accepting the invitation, but somehow her evening with Len had strengthened her resolve to remain free of the temptation of a reconciliation with Philip which such a holiday occasion as Thanksgiving might prompt.

"Are you sure, Mom?" Daniel asked, leaving Cindy waiting at the elevator and returning to the apartment door.

"I'm sure," Lorna said. "Now get out of here, all of you."

"Okay. I'll have them home Sunday night, but early," Philip said. "Probably by five o'clock."

"Okay. Fine. And Philip, this is something you

need to look at, but please don't open it until after
you're at Howard's and have at least one drink
under your belt." Lorna handed him Cindy's
report card that she had camouflaged in a plain
manila envelope.

"What is it?"

"You'll find out soon enough," Lorna said.

"Okay." He tucked the envelope into the outside pocket of his leather overnight bag. "I'll open
it at Howard's. Have a pleasant weekend, Lorna.
Do you . . . do you have any plans?"

"I . . . yes. Yes, I do," Lorna lied. "Now get
out of here."

"Okay."

Philip took a step toward the elevator, and
Lorna closed the apartment door. She leaned
against it for a moment, fighting the desire to cry,
before she looked around at her empty living
room.

"Hi, are you up to your ears in turkey?"

"No, I . . . who . . . ?" Lorna turned over and
glanced at the bedside clock. It was only a little
after eleven, although she had been in bed for
more than an hour. Even though Len had not
identified himself, Lorna recognized his voice.

"My, you're talkative this evening," Len said.

"I haven't had a very good day," Lorna confessed. "Philip had the children this year for
Thanksgiving."

"Ye gads! Have you spent the whole day
alone?"

"No, no, of course not," Lorna said. "I
had . . . I had dinner with friends and. . . . Yes. I

spent the day alone. I didn't even go out. I did some laundry, and I read for a while, and I by golly got my fill of feeling sorry for myself."

"Want some company for a nightcap?"

Lorna sat up, pulling the sheet and blankets around her. "I'm not dressed," she said, then nearly bit her tongue for the inanity of the remark.

Len laughed. "Too bad," he said. "And I wouldn't even have time to do anything about it. I just drove our guests back into the city, and I hadn't planned to do anything but call to wish you a happy Thanksgiving, but I've got half an hour if you—"

"Yes," Lorna said, already throwing back the covers and getting up. "Yes, that would be very nice."

Lorna used the intercom to alert the doorman that Len was arriving. Then she hastily dressed in comfortable plaid slacks and a loose man-tailored cotton shirt. She was amused to realize that a small part of her considered dressing like a siren, donning the fawn brown silk-and-ecru-lace nightgown and negligee Philip had given her for their seventh wedding anniversary, but it was a fleeting thought not to be taken seriously.

When the doorbell rang she was in the kitchen preparing a fresh pot of coffee.

"Hi," Len said. He was wearing a wicked smile, and Lorna could feel herself responding to it.

"Hi," she said.

"Nice place." His hand made a wide, sweeping gesture to include the carefully furnished living room with its wall of floor-to-ceiling bookcases, its huge windows with the East River view, the whole of it, with the emphasis on wood and small prints, giving a surprising country ambience for a New York apartment.

"A lot of furniture I picked up at antique shops and auctions while Philip and I were living at the shore," Lorna said. "I went through a period when I was into refinishing and upholstering."

"It shows," Len said. "You always did have good taste."

"No thanks to Mildred," Lorna said, surprised to realize that a strong touch of bitterness sounded in her voice. Her mother had a penchant for knickknacks, dust-collectors. During the early years of her marriage to Philip, Mildred had attempted to give Lorna numerous useless gifts reflecting her own taste which Lorna refused to accept. The situation had culminated in a scene of anger and bitterness.

"May I?" Len asked, taking off his coat.

Lorna laughed. "Sure." She took his coat and hung it in the closet. "I've made a pot of coffee."

"I know. Smells good."

"There's brandy, if you'd like."

"I'd like."

Soon they were settled at opposite ends of the upholstered couch. Lorna settled back against the arm, drawing her feet up beneath her. Len took a deep whiff of the cognac, gave a nod of approval, took a sip, then placed the snifter on the coffee table and also leaned back, loosening his tie and relaxing. There was something so confident about his gestures that Lorna could feel her breath catch in her throat.

"I made a pig of myself," Len said. "Overate. Drank too much. I was glad our friends decided to take me up on what was really no more than a polite offer of a ride. It got me out of the house, got my head cleared a bit. I like to drink, but I really don't like getting drunk. It's not my style."

"Nor mine," Lorna said.

And then they were both laughing, partially because of memories, partially because it was obvious that the tension Lorna had felt from the instant Len had first reappeared in her life was somehow gone this evening.

Len reached out and casually placed a hand on Lorna's knee. "It's good to hear you laugh like that," he said. "Your laugh hasn't changed, you know. The sound of it. It still has a kind of unexpected deep dark shading to it."

"Oh? Are you trying to say that it's sinister?"

"Sure. Anything that captivating has to be sinister."

"Sweet talk. Sweet talk. You know what they say about that."

"That it will get me anywhere?" Len asked.

Just as quickly as that, the lightness evaporated; a change of mood had occurred within Len. Lorna could see it on his face. His eyelids narrowed imperceptibly; there was a change in the set of his lips. The feel of his hand on her knee was no longer light and gentle, although the pressure of it had not really altered. There was, in that moment, Lorna knew, the chance for her to assume control, to divert him and defuse the situation. But she was incapable of movement, just as she had been incapable of preventing the chain of events which had brought Len here to her apartment—her empty apartment.

"Would a kiss feel good?"

"No. Yes." Was that her voice in the silence of the room?

Then his lips were on hers, merely brushing, like the hot warm caress of a summer's breeze. It was memory and reality blending in the spark of a rekindled fire . . . the touch caused her to close her eyes. There was color behind her lids, an explosion of burnt oranges and desert pinks in the soft black void, of warm rusts and auburn the color of Margot Skillen's hair. . . .

Lorna pulled away, although it felt like denying herself the warmth of the sun on a frigid day.

"Don't," Len said. "Please don't."

He had merely leaned across the space that separated them to kiss her. Now he slid across the cushions. His hands were on her shoulders as they had been the day on the library steps, but her legs were still tucked beneath her, a position that kept him from embracing her easily.

Deftly, he rearranged her body to suit him—to suit them both—and she could offer no more resistance than a doll with movable limbs.

She was in his arms, and he was murmuring her name against the skin of her neck, and she was drowning in the feel of him. Their clothes mingled in a heap on the floor. She was ready for him, although she did not understand how that could have happened, and at last, as he entered her, she knew the bittersweet joy of a dream fulfilled.

Chapter Eleven

THEIRS BECAME A LUNCHTIME AFFAIR.

They met when they could.

Because Len seemed so sure of himself when calling her at Willet's to set up meetings, Lorna suspected that he had had similar arrangements with other women in the past, but she did not question him about it.

It was understood from the beginning that her children were to be kept in the dark, although several times Cindy asked questions which made Lorna believe she suspected that something was happening which Lorna was not telling her about.

There was, of course, no way for Lorna to completely hide the change in her mood, and she did not really attempt to do that. She found herself singing again occasionally, as she had often done when she was married to Philip. She realized with a start one evening when she was helping Cindy with an English assignment that, perhaps, to some extent she *was* responsible for the dramatic drop in Cindy's grades during the past year. Neither she nor Philip had ever done the children's homework for them, but while they were still married they had both taken the time to review assignments periodically, offering advice and pointing out areas where improvement would show. Now Lorna rarely had the energy to do this.

"There really is a difference between helping and simply yelling at her to get the work done," Lorna said to Beth. "This week we've been working on punctuation. It isn't that she doesn't know what has to be done," Lorna said. "She writes like Philip does. She gets her ideas out first—they're original and interesting—and be damned with the punctuation and spelling. But without Philip here to give her the example of going back and polishing the material after the creative work is done, she just hasn't been bothering with that step. I've been so wrapped up in myself, my own problems, that I wasn't taking the time."

"It's important that you realized that," Beth said. "It ought to help."

"Yes, I think so."

It was not until the second week in December, after Lorna had seen Len three or four more times, that she told Beth. She had to tell someone. She wanted to share her happiness even if it was tempered with the pain of knowing that Len was married and the time they spent together would always be severely limited.

"I'm glad," Beth said. "You need someone—a man in your life. It *is* difficult, getting emotionally involved with a married man, but it's no more difficult than battling the emotional problems that stem from no physical contact with any man. Look at yourself, Lorna. You're smiling again. Your sense of humor is beginning to return. It shows on your face."

"Yes, I know," Lorna said. "Some part of me gets angry about it, too. Why does it have to be having a man in my life instead of something I've *accomplished.*"

"Don't be a jerk, Lorna. You *have* accomplished something. You've seen yourself through a difficult divorce; you're working at a job you like; you're doing fine by your kids. I think women get brainwashed into thinking that managing time for an affair isn't an accomplishment with all the other things we have to do to keep ourselves going."

"Yes," Lorna said. "I think you're right about that. Because it does take a lot of time, and it takes commitment, too. I've never done this before, so I didn't realize that. It's not the same kind of a commitment I made to my marriage, but it has involved some conscious decisions, and it does mean rearranging my time. Little things. Like putting off errands for a different day. We've only seen each other a few times so far, and I still haven't gotten used to the idea of meeting someone just to make love either."

"Relax, Lorna," Beth said. "Relax and enjoy it. Please don't let yourself complicate something that's really simple."

"Okay," Lorna said. "I'll try."

After so many years of marriage, and more than a year of living alone, it seemed as if Beth was right and that it should be a simple element Lorna was adding to her life—a man who seemed to care about her, who made her laugh, who made love to her and made her feel like a woman again.

No, Lorna thought. That wasn't right. She had spent this past year feeling all too much like a woman, a trapped woman, a woman caught in a pervasive and difficult situation.

But it was easier now for her to get up in the morning than it was before Len . . . before she had a *lover* in her life.

Not that having a lover fit into any of the preconceptions of such a situation which she had formed from magazine fiction and television. She and Len rarely spent the little time they managed to find for each other anywhere except in her apartment. Even then, until they were safely inside with the door locked behind them, Lorna was unable to relax. Len had stopped in unexpectedly at Willet's and suggested their first lunchtime tryst at her apartment. It had taken Lorna most of the time they had together to recover from the uneasiness she experienced when the doorman had simply glanced at Len while greeting her. What must he think? she had wondered. She belatedly repeated this question to Beth.

Beth laughed. "He gets paid not to wonder about things like that," Beth said. "Really, Lorna. I'm sorry if it sounds condescending, but sometimes you're amusingly naive. If it bothers you, give the day man an extra ten bucks for Christmas next week."

This time Lorna laughed. "It doesn't bother me *that* much," she said.

But as Christmas—and her one-month anniversary of intimacy with Len—drew closer, Lorna began to experience what Beth called the "holiday season blues."

For Christmas week, Len and Margot were taking their children to Colorado to ski, and Philip was taking Cindy and Daniel to his parents' winter place in West Palm Beach. Mildred had invited

Lorna home to Buffalo for Christmas, but she declined the invitation.

On Monday night, a week before Christmas, Lorna arrived home to find the table in the dining alcove set for two. There were candles and a bottle of Moët & Chandon chilling in the silver-plated ice bucket Mildred once had given her as an anniversary present. It had belonged to her maternal grandmother, whom Lorna had never known because she had died when Lorna was an infant. The ice bucket was one of the few things Mildred had ever given Lorna which she was pleased to have, although she used it rarely these days.

Philip was standing in the door to the kitchen, a canvas cook's apron around him, a wire whisk in his hand. There was a look of naked pleading on his face, a look which said, *"Please,* please let me do this."

Lorna bit off an angry line which threatened to escape her and nodded a silent greeting. She did not want this reminder of the past comfortable intimacy which had existed between her and Philip. It carried the aura of temptation with it, and right now that was not what she needed, although if someone had asked her what she *did* need at that moment, she knew she would have been unable to articulate an answer.

She took off her coat and hung it in the closet. The sound of television was muted as the door to the den was closed. Obviously, whatever surprise had occasioned Philip's presence in the apartment he had already shared with Daniel and Cindy, and they were cooperating in his attempt to make it a celebration.

"I waited for you," he said. "Would you like the dessert soufflé flavored with Grand Marnier or coffee?"

Lorna checked the bottle of champagne. It was one of the few bottles remaining from a case they had been given as an anniversary present three years before.

"Grand Marnier," she said, "of course."

"Of course." Philip smiled broadly and bowed from the waist, using the whisk like a feather cap to complete a courtier's salute.

Lorna's heart turned over. You just don't turn it off, she thought. The feelings change, and shift from love to anger, and then mellow around the edges. What she had felt for Philip, the love she had had for this man, was always different from the love she had felt—that she now felt again—for Len. Feelings of great intensity were rarely sexual in the same way. When she wanted Philip it was rarely wanting in the sense of making love, but in the sense of making play.

"What's the occasion?" Lorna asked, keeping her tone light.

"You are looking at the man who has written the Book-of-the-Month Club selection for July," Philip said.

"Oh, that's wonderful!"

"And Brockton's going to reissue my first three books in an omnibus volume. That's going to be offered also."

There was boyish charm mingled with continuing disbelief on Philip's face.

"You've earned it, Philip. I'm very happy for you."

"Thanks." He retrieved a half pitcher of Bloody

Marys from the refrigerator. "Just the way you like them . . . very spicy and not too much vodka."

"Well, it hasn't been that long," Lorna said. "It shouldn't have taxed your memory too much to remember the recipe." There was an edge in her voice which surprised her; she could see Philip react to it, but consciously push it aside in favor of continuing the scenario he had written for the evening.

"It didn't," Philip said. "But we're going to have a Caesar salad without anchovies. I couldn't find any in the cabinet, and I forgot them at the store."

"Well, that's easy," Lorna said, forcing herself to pick up Philip's mood. It was infinitely preferable to her own. She had expected a call from Len during the day which had not come, and she was disappointed and angry with herself because of it. "Just serve the salad, and we'll christen it with a new name."

Philip poured their drinks; Lorna leaned against the refrigerator and watched Philip do the final mixing of the soufflé. When it was safely in the oven, he removed the apron, got Lorna settled in the seat she preferred at the table, and served them a delicious simple meal of salad, filet mignon pan-fried with mushrooms and shallots, and steamed green beans with a brown butter and garlic sauce.

They drank a bottle of an excellent California Cabernet Sauvignon with the meal, and opened the champagne with the dessert soufflé.

Cindy and Daniel were conspicuously absent during the meal, although once there was the sound of television channel-changing with a momentary protest from Daniel.

Philip made Turkish coffee after dinner. It had been an altogether pleasant meal.

Then Philip pulled a long white envelope from his inside pocket.

"What's this?" Lorna asked.

"It's from my mother," Philip said as he handed her the envelope.

Lorna held the envelope for a moment, looking at Ann's neat, well-formed handwriting. Then she opened it. There was an Amtrack ticket envelope, and a short note.

Dear Lorna:

I know it will not be possible for you to take the plane with Philip and the children the day before Christmas Eve because of your job, and also that you do not really like to fly. But I miss you in our lives, and so does Herb. I regret that I was unable to convince you not to go through with the divorce, but I regret even more that we somehow allowed ourselves to grow apart.

Please use the enclosed.

Love,
Ann

The "enclosed" was a round-trip train ticket for an Amtrack roomette on an afternoon train leaving New York for West Palm Beach on Christmas Day and a return reservation for the following Sunday.

During the years of their marriage, Lorna's well-known dislike of planes had often caused problems for them, because, although Philip also enjoyed the comforts of train travel, going by roomette was more expensive than flying, and they usually had given in to money pressure.

"Will you do it, Lorna?" Philip asked. "There's a lot to celebrate this year, and I know you regret having let things get out of control with Ann."

And what would I do if I stayed here? Lorna thought. Have a repeat of Thanksgiving Day, which had been horrible except for Len's unexpected arrival that night? There was no chance of a reoccurrence—he would be in Colorado with his wife and family.

"Yes," she said, making a decision. "Yes. I will. I do miss Ann, and—"

"Good," Philip said. "Good!" He rose from the table, went to the den, and opened the door. "You're mother's going to come, guys," he said to Cindy and Daniel.

"Yippee!" Daniel yelped. Immediately Cindy ran to the table. She threw her arms around Lorna. "I'm glad, Mom!" she said. "I'm really glad. You'll have a good time, and . . . I *love* you!"

"I love you, too, Cindy-Bear," Lorna said, hugging her daughter, holding her close, fighting back tears. How strange and wonderful children were, she thought; or, perhaps, what was strange was an adult's inability to find pure happiness in pleasure experienced by others.

Chapter Twelve

W HAT'S THE MATTER, LORNA?" LEN LEANED ON one elbow. His body was both soft and hard. It was as firm as Philip's, although it felt very different against her skin—more angular, more athletic. Len did not have Philip's inherent physical gracefulness but he exercised, skiied, and played tennis, and those accomplishments showed in his physique. He was also much less inhibited where lovemaking was concerned, inventive and gentle, impatient and yet maddeningly considerate. He drew things out to make sure she was satisfied, talking to her, asking her to tell him what she wanted, and being patiently amused when she was unable to articulate her thoughts about sex. She could not find the words. How could she find the words when she herself could not imagine what more she could possibly want so far as this unexpected affair was concerned? She and Philip had not talked about sex in bed either.

To distract herself from these thoughts, Lorna ran her fingers through Len's wavy hair. The gesture was a hangover from years before when she had believed it to be a sign of affection. The gesture had appeared frequently in the popular fiction she had read during her teens that had affected her greatly.

"I'm always quiet after making love," she said.

"Yes, you are."

Even as she said those words, a fog of indecision deepened in Lorna's mind. One part of her felt a strong desire to sleep, to turn her mind away from a realization that she wanted *something*, something *more*, something she could not define; another part of her felt a need to communicate. The need to sleep was related to the feelings she had been battling since Len came back into her life. The need to communicate had to do with the evening with Philip and the news of his impending success.

Is it always this way? she wondered.

Although *Clear Lake*, the novel on which Philip would, at last, make money, was being published well after their separation and divorce, Philip had started writing the book even before he had begun his affair with Sally Thornton. As had been true of his other books, much of the preliminary work had been shared with Lorna. During the middle years of their marriage, Philip had used Lorna as a sounding board and had discussed his ideas with her. He had sometimes even used sections of their own dialogue almost verbatim, putting the appropriate words into the mouths of appropriate characters. Often they had laughed about it; always, there had been a sense of sharing.

The problem of dealing with what Lorna recognized as a sense of injustice was difficult enough to come to grips with as it was; to attempt to discuss it with Len was of and in itself a problem of equally distressing proportions. It didn't seem right, somehow, to bring problems relating to a marriage that no longer existed to an affair that had barely begun.

Len kissed her lightly on the mouth and began to dress.

"I'm surprised you haven't mentioned the good news," Len said.

"About Philip's book?"

"Yes."

Lorna snuggled under the covers. "I'm ambivalent about it," she said honestly.

Len laughed. "Yes. I can see. The thought of it sends you deeper into bed."

Lorna smiled at the accuracy of Len's remark. "I suppose you've seen similar situations before."

"I have," Len said. "Will it help you at all? Philip's financial success?"

"I suppose so. Where the children are concerned. At least, in regard to creature comforts and vacations. Still, there's something about it that doesn't seem right."

Len shrugged. "That's the way of the world, woman. Now come on, lazy, get up. You have to get back to work, too. You can't afford to lose your job."

Lorna threw off the covers, straightened the bedspread and began to dress. There was something about Len's comments which annoyed her, not because he wasn't right, but because he *was* right. She didn't want to know that what she was feeling about Philip's impending success was "the way of the world, woman."

The lovemaking she shared with Len was intense and satisfying. She enjoyed Len's company before the act. Afterwards, however, he seemed to acquire a layer of brittleness, almost as if he left a part of himself behind when he shed his clothes, and acquired it again when he dressed. She liked him better without it.

"You should talk about this with a friend," Len said. "It's not an easy burden to keep on your own shoulders."

"Aren't you a friend?"

"Yes. Yes, of course. But I'm also a man, and I'm not going to give you the understanding and sympathy a woman friend would where this is concerned. I've thought about how things would work if Margot and I got divorced. It's not an easy situation."

Lorna's back was to Len, checking the collar of her blouse in the mirror to make sure it was straight. She heard his words, and found herself replaying them in her mind, looking for implications. Was he suggesting in an oblique way that he was thinking of leaving Margot? The thought made her nervous. Once before in her life she had decided not to marry Len, and her thoughts had not been running in that direction now, either.

The weather had gotten much colder, although there still had not been a snowfall. Once outside the building, Lorna pulled the collar of her serviceable black wool coat up around her neck.

"You need a scarf, Lorna," Len said.

"I know. Gloves, too. I seem to lose them more than the children do."

Len hailed a taxi on Third Avenue, dropping Lorna off on the corner of Forty-sixth and Sixth before proceeding uptown. She was back to Willet's by a few minutes after two, having extended her lunch hour by fifteen minutes. She was not in the usual good mood which her previous trysts with Len had aroused, and was surprised that the phrase "postcoital depression" cropped into her consciousness. She liked it even less when she felt a niggling annoyance because Len could afford to take a taxi to and from his office and she could not. With a certainty she didn't like, Lorna realized that she was being caught in a different kind of a trap, one for which she could not define the parameters because she could not focus on an issue that was beyond her experience.

On Saturday, Beth and Lorna spent the morning in Beth's apartment. Philip was leaving for Florida with Cindy and Daniel Tuesday night, a day before the official school vacation began. Since Lorna was also leaving for Florida later in the week, she did not feel the need to do her usual grocery shopping.

"I've still got presents to buy!" Beth said. "You've got it all taken care of, haven't you?"

"Yes," Lorna said. "I've been shopping at break time. It helps keep me occupied. Cindy and Daniel are out doing the rest of their shopping now. Philip gave them each money for presents to supplement what I gave them and what they had saved from their allowances. This year, I decided to let them do their shopping without me because they asked to."

"That's a good idea," Beth said. "Cindy's certainly old enough and very responsible, and Daniel has a good sense of what people he knows like. Sometimes, I think both of your children were born adult."

"You wouldn't say that if you saw the way they were carrying on about the trip to Florida," Lorna said. "Their grandparents have promised them a day at Disney World this trip. You'd think they were both six years old, although I have to confess that I wouldn't mind going myself."

"Are you packed?"

"No, but that won't take long. I'm only going to be gone for a few days. I'm just taking a couple of bathing suits, some sportswear, and what I wear on the train. Ann likes to go out, so I suppose that means one night at a good restaurant. But I'm really planning just to relax and get some sun and swimming in."

"Sounds wonderful," Beth said.

"Yes. Yes. It does."

"What's bothering you, Lorna? You should be perky and happy, and you're moping around like you've lost a friend. Are you and Len having problems?"

"No. I saw him this week. I saw Philip, too. He came over unexpectedly and cooked dinner for me."

"I know. Cindy told Dawn."

"His new book is going to be a Book-of-the-Month Club selection."

"That's wonderful."

"It's wonderful, and it's also part of the problem," Lorna said. "Oh, Lord, Beth, I'm really feeling trapped," Lorna said. "Philip's going to make a lot of money, and I feel as if I should share in that somehow, but it wasn't a possibility we discussed during our divorce settlement. The other day, after Len and I made love, he dropped me back off at work in a taxi and it made me angry because I can't afford cabs. I'm involved in an affair with a married man—whom I don't want to marry even if he were free—and I can't see a future for myself except one that's a treading-water situation every day."

It was late in the afternoon before Lorna had talked out her problems with Beth to the point where her mood began to shift, but even so there was a lingering depression that melded with her usual Saturday night doldrums. She spent the evening wrapping the presents she had purchased for Christmas, carefully packing them in her light-weight parachute-cloth bag for the trip to Florida. Cindy and Daniel were doing the same in the den, making a cheerful secret out of what they had bought and what they were doing. Slowly the sounds of their laughing and bickering began to alter Lorna's mood. She had left the present she had bought for Len to the last—a beautifully hand-tooled leather eyeglass case that matched the leather of his briefcase. It was a present she was not sure she was going to give—one which had cost her more money than she should have spent. Lorna went to the den and pushed the door open.

"Hey, you can't come in, Mom," Cindy said. "I'm not finished yet!" Cindy pushed a box under the sofa bed.

"This one's for you, Mom," Daniel said, holding up a square package wrapped in a double layer of bright red paper with a big, awkwardly tied silver bow. "I wrapped it first."

"You're both doing a good job," Lorna said, looking at the snips of paper and odd bits of ribbon which littered the den floor. She squelched an urge to yell at them to tidy up the room. "Do you want some help?"

"I don't," Cindy said.

"I do," Daniel said. "Any suggestions for this? I got it for Grandma Mildred." He held up a tulip-shaped milk-glass bowl and a box of After Eight chocolate-covered mints, one of Mildred's few sweet-tooth indulgences. "She *is* going to like this, isn't she? I can't figure out how to wrap them. They didn't have a box for the bowl in the store."

Cindy held up a package wrapped in green foil and tied with a piece of thick knotted white yarn. "I got her a companion piece," she said. "Daniel spotted the bowl first, though, I've got to admit. Grandma Mildred is always the hardest to shop for. She's got so many *things*. Do you think we can find a box to pack these in so we can send them to Buffalo and they won't break in the mail?"

"Yes, of course, we can," Lorna said. "Why don't you try wrapping the bowl like Cindy did, Dan? Just put paper around it and bring the edges up and tie it with a ribbon. You can wrap the mints separately and put cards on both of them . . . 'Open me first,' and 'Open me second.'"

"Hey, that's a good idea!"

"I think I saved a box that will be just perfect," Lorna said. She went to the utility closet in the hallway and rummaged until she found what she was looking for, a small heavy carton just the right size.

It was nearly midnight before the children had finished wrapping their presents and the gifts for Mildred were safely tucked into the carton for mailing. Cindy had put a rock-and-roll station on

the stereo instead of turning on television, and
Lorna realized that her children's infectious good
mood had helped her to relax. She was sitting on
the floor of the den, as they were, using the sofa
bed as a backrest, her legs stretched out in front of
her. Debris from the present-wrapping chores was
everywhere, and she didn't even care. It was only
a ten-minute job to straighten up, and, on an
impulse, because a Beatles' song she particularly
liked was playing, Lorna got up and began to
dance.

For a few minutes, Cindy and Daniel chided her
good-naturedly, then they, too, got up and shared
in the impromptu dancing, kicking the scraps of
paper and the scissors and the ribbons out of the
way, laughing and swaying, finally joining hands
and moving to the rhythms of the music.

All too soon, the song ended.

Lorna gathered her children into her arms.
"This has been fun, hasn't it?" she asked. "It's the
nicest evening I've had in a long time."

"Nicer than the evening with Dad?" Daniel
asked, his voice carrying a tone of disbelief.

"Well. . . ." Caught by surprise, Lorna realized
that she would be lying if she answered a simple
yes to Daniel's question. The evening with Philip
. . . was it the fun of it that was at the core of what
was bothering her? The intolerable fact that he
had wanted to share his news with her the way he
had? That the sharing was incomplete, incomplete
for both of them?

Firmly, she pushed her children away from her,
pulling Cindy back for one last-minute hug, then
pushing the inevitable lock of hair back from
Daniel's forehead.

"It's late," she said. "Off to bed with both of you."

"We have to clean up, Mom," Cindy said. "We shouldn't leave this mess for you." There was a look of comprehension on Cindy's face that was so adult and compassionate that Lorna could feel tears forming, so close to the surface she was not sure she could keep them from showing.

"Okay," she said, bolting for the door. "I'm going to bed. I'll see you in the morning."

"Good night, Mom. I love you," Cindy said.

"Me, too," Daniel said.

Chapter Thirteen

THROUGH THE EARLY MORNING MIST, THE TRAIN clanked its way toward Palm Beach, *ker-chug, ker-chug, ker-chug,* the sound lulling Lorna into a sense of peace. Where were they? she wondered. The window in the roomette was a vista to a land she associated with fairy tales: soft gray-green trees and vegetation foreign to her eyes; the nearly full-sized bed that, during the day, was hidden behind the comfortable couchlike red plush seat was a reminder of childhood when she would creep into her parents' bed early on Sunday mornings. Lorna remembered those mornings, even if, for reasons she did not understand, Mildred denied her the right to the memories. Her mother had claimed once that she had never allowed *her* child to invade the privacy of the bedroom she shared with her husband.

There was Spanish moss growing on trees; there were palmetto fronds, and occasional patches of flowers. Sometime during the night, the train had passed through the twilight zone that separates the North from the South.

The train rounded a curve, and passed a sign with faded lettering announcing Ponce de Leon's Fountain of Youth.

Florida.

They were somewhere in northern Florida.

Soon, too soon, the train ride would end, and there would be three days to spend with Philip, the children, and Philip's parents, Ann and Herb. Well, she would get through, Lorna thought. Again, her eyes were drawn to the window, although it was really the comfort of the bed, the luxuriousness of the surroundings that she particularly liked about the train ride.

She stretched, plumped up the pillow, and rearranged herself. The magical quality of the landscape began to disappear with the lifting of the early morning fog. Factory buildings, jerry-built houses, and the inevitable trackside debris of discarded beer cans, soda bottles, and papers began to catch her attention.

She was glad when the porter knocked on her door, announcing that the dining car had begun serving breakfast.

A few hours later, the train pulled into Lorna's stop. She tipped the porter, and disembarked onto the platform. Philip and the children were waiting for her at the far end of the station.

"You're only twelve minutes late!" Daniel said, proudly holding up a Timex for Lorna to inspect. "Isn't it super! Grandma and Grandpa gave it to me for Christmas."

"Me, too," Cindy said, also displaying a watch.

Lorna hugged her children, and handed Philip her baggage check.

"Mom and Dad are back at the condo," Philip said.

"I'm looking forward to seeing them."

It was pleasantly warm, not outlandishly hot, and there was a soft wind blowing. The air smelled fresh and very clean, and seemed to caress her skin.

"Oh, Lord, I've got a sudden yen for about three dozen oranges!" Lorna said. "And a gallon of grapefruit juice!"

"We went to Disney World just like we were promised, and it was terrific. You would have liked it!" Daniel said. Already he had started to get a fine tan, and he wore a smile that looked permanent. Cindy was getting a tan, too, and a smidgen of freckles had begun to appear across her nose.

"Yesterday, we made a trip to an orchard," Cindy said. "They had a funny little train, and they took us through the whole place."

"There were all kinds of trees and flowers, and, you know what?" Daniel said. "Amos and Andy own part of it."

"No, that's not exactly right," Philip said, "but we can go into that later. I'm going to go get the luggage. Take your mom to the car, kids."

"Sure, Dad," Cindy said. She took Lorna's hand. "Come on, we're parked over here. You know, we ought to come down here sometime in February or March," Cindy said. "The people at the orchard said they grew strawberries like this!" Cindy held her hands apart to indicate a berry the size of a grapefruit, and Lorna laughed.

"That's the trouble with sunshine," she said. "It makes everything seem very big."

Twenty minutes later they were in the apartment in the condominium building. The greetings for the first meeting with her former in-laws in more than a year, which Lorna had worried might be strained, proved warm and friendly and, fifteen minutes later, she was indulging in her third orange.

That afternoon, she went to the pool with Cindy and Daniel, and, by the second morning, Lorna was feeling truly relaxed. She had always liked Philip's parents, and their sincere pleasure at having her visit with them again showed. On Lorna's second night in Florida, they dined at an excellent seafood restaurant. Afterwards, with Cindy and Daniel watching over their shoulders, the adults played six rubbers of bridge, another pleasure which Lorna had not indulged in since her separation and divorce from Philip.

By the third morning, Lorna had acquired the start of a real tan, and a deep reluctance to return to New York.

It was so easy.

The tempo was so unhurried.

There was a relief in picking up routines which had their roots established many years before.

Philip was in a fine mood, working four hours each morning, polishing the completed draft of his new novel, anticipating an enjoyable year ahead.

Everything was fine, indeed—except that Lorna was sleeping alone for the first time under the same roof with Philip. And she missed Len.

Or maybe what she missed was Philip.

That idea, and that idea alone, was the single disturbing element in the otherwise exceedingly pleasant break from her routine.

On her fourth morning, the day she was to leave, that realization occurred to her in a form she would have been capable of articulating only to Beth. It caused her to rise early. She was sharing a bedroom with Cindy; Philip and Daniel were sleeping on the sofa bed in the living room. Hurriedly, Lorna pulled on her bathing suit, and, careful not to make unnecessary noise, she left the apartment and headed for the swimming pool.

There were others at the pool, even though it was not yet nine o'clock—the granddaughter of the couple who had the apartment next to Philip's parents, an unhappy teenager getting over her first excursion into love, was swimming desperate laps; an older woman, who Lorna recognized from previous visits although they had never spoken, was kicking her legs for exercise in the shallow end of the pool, her arms hooked over the edge of the spill ledge.

Lorna left her terry-cloth robe on a chair, tucked her hair into a bathing cap, dove into the water and began swimming laps. She had never gone in much for exercise, although she enjoyed swimming. With an effort of will, she concentrated on her breathing. She had spent the night plagued by thoughts she did not want to have in her head. She wasn't ready to go back! She didn't want to go back to New York, not to her apartment, not to her job at Willet's, and not to the structure of her affair with Len which was different from the lovemaking with him! Years ago, after she and Philip sold the house on the Jersey shore, they had decided to move south as soon as Philip made money from his books.

And now he was going to, and now they were no longer *they!*

It wasn't that she wanted to give up Len, either.

What it amounted to was that she had two men in her life, and she didn't really have either of them.

There was a splash, the sound of someone diving into the pool, and, unexpectedly, Lorna was pulled under the surface of the water. It was the kind of playful attack she had not experienced since she was a child, and when she surfaced, sputtering and annoyed and, at the same time, aware of some strange pleasure at having been singled out by someone who wanted to play with her, she discovered that it was Philip.

"Good morning," he said, dunking her again.

When she came up for air, despite herself, Lorna's mouth screwed up into a fiercesome grimace. Without conscious thought she splashed water into Philip's face. Then her hands reached for his shoulders, ducking him under the water in return.

She was pulled under again herself. Somehow, legs got tangled. Somehow, she was in his arms. Somehow, he was kissing her and she was responding. She wanted him! Then! There! Always!

She pulled away, managed to get free, swam with a sense of desperate purpose to the side of the pool, and attempted to pull herself out.

116

Her muscles were out of shape, and she could not manage the maneuver in a single fluid motion.

Philip reached her side and restrained her easily.

"Don't, Lorna. Don't. I'm sorry."

"There's nothing to be sorry for." Lorna turned her head away. "I . . . it felt good," she said. "It's been a long while since someone felt like playing with me, and . . . it felt good."

"It's just that . . . it's been so nice seeing you unwind the last couple of days," Philip said. "We're over the worst of it now. It's time we should be friends again."

This last, on Philip's part, was said with an edge of pleading to it. Lorna responded with a smile.

"Yes," she said. "You're right. But let's . . . let's not do it around the kids, okay? I wouldn't want them—"

"You wouldn't want them to get the wrong idea, right?"

"That's right."

The sudden hardness in Philip's tone of voice made Lorna aware that it was not as warm as she had thought, even though she was in Florida. For a second, she remained undecided, then she pushed off from the side of the pool and continued swimming. She could feel Philip's eyes on her. Then he was swimming by her side, matching her stroke for stroke.

She speeded up.

He speeded up.

She slowed down.

He did the same.

She finished five laps; six. With an effort, she started the seventh, then headed for the ladder at the far end of the pool, hauling herself up by the guard rails. Her legs felt heavy—but not as heavy as the turmoil raging inside her.

She pulled off her bathing cap and toweled dry by the side of the beach chair where she had left her things; ten minutes later she headed back to the apartment.

Philip was still in the pool, swimming laps.

Chapter Fourteen

THINGS WERE DIFFERENT AFTER HER HOLIDAY, even though the routine of work was the same except for the impending departure of Gail from Willet's. Fortunately, Beth's ex-husband had found a job for Gail in one of his stores as he had promised. Gail would begin work there the week following her last week at Willet's. Lorna was going to miss her. Gail had been a friend—someone Lorna could talk to during the day. And, until a new routine was established, it was going to be harder for Lorna to meet Len at lunchtime with peace of mind with one less employee to tend the store in her absence.

The physical attraction she felt for Len had not lessened at all, and thoughts of their lovemaking still sprang into her mind at the most unexpected times, thoughts that were capable of exciting her beyond reason. But Lorna was also aware of the lack of nonsexual play in their relationship in a way she had not been before the disturbing episode in the pool with Philip.

During the long night ride on the train returning from Florida, she had luxuriated in the comfort of purposeful aloneness, turning away a quite determined attempt at conversation from a distinguished older man from Philadelphia. He had shared the table with her at dinner, and he also was traveling in the sleeping car section. But Lorna politely declined his invitation for an after-dinner cordial in the parlor car.

The evening had given Lorna another chance to think freely. She let her thoughts drift, concentrating on snatches of memories, piecing them together as they surfaced into a crazy quilt. This kaleidoscope of past and present led to a realization that, for a second time, she could picture no life, no future with Len. She realized this was not altogether fair because the reality of their situation did not leave room for the kind of talking and courting which might have made such a life possible. But, also for a second time, she felt the strong, playful presence of Philip in her life—Philip not as her ex-husband, but Philip as a man.

It was very disturbing.

Over and over, she played back the scene in the swimming pool; over and over, she played back the remark Len had made about the thoughts he had had in regard to what would happen if he and Margot divorced. She hoped that Len's remarks had been idle speculation. For the present, she was quite content with the situation—no, not content. "Resigned" was a better word.

Lorna had less time than she wanted with her

lover; still, she did not want him to be anything but her lover. As to Philip, there was nothing to do in any event. They were tied together by the children and by the past. With a sense of firm resolve, she put all thoughts of the possibility of the resumption of anything more intimate between them out of her mind as she had done several times in the past months.

On New Year's Eve, there was a party at Beth's. Shortly before seven o'clock, Lorna dressed in a long black pleated skirt and a black silk mantailored blouse made ultra feminine by being shot through with gold and silver threads. After buckling on her high-heeled strap-back silver shoes, she took the elevator down to Beth's apartment on the eleventh floor to help with last-minute preparations.

"You look absolutely gorgeous!" Beth said. "I love your outfit. How'd you get such a wonderful tan in only a couple of days? I'm jealous!"

"I worked at it," Lorna said. "I tan easily, you know that. A half hour three times a day and some terrific lotion Ann got for me."

"You look relaxed, too, I'm glad to see. You really didn't have to come down so early. Willemina's here. But I'm glad you did. I still haven't decided if I should wear a dress, or those wild lounging pajamas I got last week. You haven't seen them yet. They're a leopard pattern, but with a lot of red and orange in addition to the browns and black. Come on. Be an angel. Help me choose."

"Sure."

An hour later, Beth was wearing a flattering, yet very conservative beige dress. Lorna had given her honest opinion about the lounging pajamas—the print was too big for Beth to carry off at her height. Beth was still sitting in front of her vanity table mirror working on her makeup. Lorna was sitting on a pink velvet upholstered chair near the table, listening to Beth prattle on about the guests who were coming to the party. She felt relaxed now, after years of friendship, with Beth's haphazard, whirlwind approach to a social evening in her home. Four or five outfits in addition to the lounging outfit had been tried on, discarded, and remained jumbled on the bed. Beth was experimenting with her third shade of eyeshadow. In another few minutes, Lorna knew from experience, Beth would jump up, announce that work had to be done in the kitchen, and Willemina would come and tidy up the bedroom while Beth made additional disorder in the kitchen.

"I didn't realize the party was going to be so big tonight," Lorna said. "You really didn't talk about it at all to me before I went away."

"Only thirty-five people," Beth said.

"Do I know any of them? So far, all you've mentioned are people I don't know."

"Sure, you know some of them."

At the party Lorna met a man named Mike Bishop, a widower in his mid-forties who had lost his wife and two children several years before in an automobile accident. He was slightly over six feet tall, had a small, brush-type moustache, and had a pleasant, ruddy complexion which made Lorna suspect that he took frequent walks out of doors. His suit was well-cut, but the jacket was a shade too large; obviously, he had taken off weight since the previous winter and had not bothered to have his clothes altered. He looked like the certified public accountant that he was and had a quiet way of speaking and a shy air. About eleven o'clock, realizing that they were gracing opposite corners of the living room, and had been doing so since early in the evening, they drifted together and found talking easy. At midnight, they kissed. Lorna enjoyed it. It was the kiss of a friend, newfound and well-met, leaving the possibilities of anything else to be discovered later.

About one o'clock, as the party began to thin out, one of Beth's guests suggested that they head for a jazz club in So-Ho. Beth thought it was a good idea.

"Do you want to go, too?" Mike Bishop asked. "I haven't heard live music for a long time."

"Neither have I," Lorna confessed.

"Okay. Let's do it," Mike said.

"Okay!"

There were ten of them—five couples—who decided to go. They had some difficulty finding taxis, but soon they were all settled and driving along streets that were well-peopled with noisy and excited New Year's Eve revelers.

"I can't remember the last time I was out so late," Lorna said to Mike.

"It's been awhile for me, too," he said.

The jazz club was located in a block of warehouses and living lofts in lower Manhattan in an area of the city with which Lorna was not familiar. She had come with Mike and Beth and her date and the other acquaintances from Beth's party with no preconception of the club in her mind. So she was surprised at how attractively it was decorated and how intimate the ambience was, even though they entered directly into the barroom.

There was a wait for tables for the next set, but there was room at the long bar. Beveled mirror sections behind the bar made this entry room seem more spacious than it was. The walls were paneled with a light-colored beautifully grained wood, and huge earthenware vases filled with tall willowy ferns were placed in strategic places. It was a splendid visual and tactile change from the cold winter outside.

The stage could be seen from the bar. A seven-piece jazz band was playing up-tempo music; the audience in the music room was attentive, applauding solos vigorously.

The bartender came to take their order.

The music was happy and infectious.

"I'm glad we came," Lorna said. "This is fun!"

"Yes," Mike agreed. "I'm sorry there isn't any place to dance, though. That would be great, too."

"Yes," Lorna agreed. "It would be fun."

"If you want to dance, I have some friends who live near here in a huge loft," Beth said. "They are having a party tonight, too. I'm sure it will be going on until dawn. We could go there after the set."

"That's a good idea," Mike said.

"Let's see how we feel then," Lorna said.

"Okay."

But it was nearly three-thirty when the next set was finished, and although the music was wonderful—a combination of ballads and bebop, with excellent solos all around, particularly by the trombone player and the bassist—Lorna was not really in the mood to extend the evening.

"I've had enough of New Year's," she said to Mike.

There was an awkward moment then. Lorna could see Beth smiling, wondering how Lorna was going to handle the remainder of the evening because Beth and the others still had some energy and were going to head on to the loft party to dance.

"What if I find us a cab and drop you off back at your apartment?" Mike asked. "I've had enough revelry tonight, too."

"All right," Lorna said.

As luck would have it, a taxi bringing several other musicians with their instruments pulled up to the jazz club as they were leaving. The group was obviously ready to join in the fun and turn the last set of the evening at the club into an all-night jam session. Lorna and Mike took the vacant cab.

The taxi ride uptown to Lorna's building caused her some concern. Mike Bishop was pleasant, and the evening had been fun. She was relaxed but she was also aware of the slightly disturbing hope that Mike was going to make a pass at her. She was in the mood to take a risk and go along with it, curious about what it would feel like. What bothered her was that it was not any real feeling for Mike which prompted this almost conscious decision but the curious thought that perhaps making love with another man might help her find a perspective where Len was concerned. However, there was something about Mike which clearly indicated that he was looking for a serious relationship. *That* was frightening, but not the thought of physical intimacy with a new man.

As the taxi pulled into her block, Lorna gathered courage to instigate things herself, to ask Mike up for a drink, but she hesitated just long enough to lose the opportunity.

The cab pulled to a stop. Before Lorna could find words to prolong the evening, Mike leaned over and asked the driver to wait.

"I'm going to walk the lady to the door," he said, "then I'd like to go on uptown."

He gave the driver an address on the upper West Side in the Seventies. It was not too far from where Philip lived, and it made Lorna realize that she had, indeed, put aside thoughts of her complicated personal life for almost the entire evening or, at least, for that part of the evening she had spent in Mike's easygoing presence.

"Thank you, Mike," Lorna said after he helped her out of the cab and walked her to the front door of the building, holding the lobby door open. "This has been very pleasant. I really had a good time."

"It's all right. I had just as good a time as you did, I'm sure." He started to turn away, and Lorna was surprised that a real sense of disappointment touched her. Then he stopped. "Are you listed in the phone book?" he asked.

"Yes. Yes, I am," Lorna said.

"Good, then I'll give you a call in a few days, unless you'll say yes now to having dinner with me this weekend."

"I . . . I'm not sure," Lorna said, hesitating.

"What about next week?"

"No," Lorna said, "it isn't that. I'll be pleased to see you again. It's just that my children are due back later in the week, and I'm not free to make plans until I talk to them. They're old enough for me to leave them alone now when I go out, but I've got to crosscheck schedules and get them settled back in."

"I understand," Mike said. "Look, what would you say if we made things tentative for next Friday? We can change the date to another night if that proves inconvenient?"

"All right," Lorna agreed. "All right. That sounds okay."

"Fine. Shall we say seven, or is that too early?"

"Yes, a little," Lorna said. "Seven-thirty would be more convenient. It would give me time to unwind a bit after work."

"All right. Seven-thirty it is. I'll call you later in the week to confirm." Then Mike kissed the back of her hand, such an old-fashioned and yet appropriate gesture for the moment that Lorna did not check her impulse to lean over and kiss him on the cheek.

"I'll look forward to it," she said.

"Good night, Lorna."

"Good night."

Lorna stood in the entranceway to the building and watched Mike's taxi drive off. And so it was that she was still in the lobby waiting for the elevator when the taxi bringing Sally Thornton home from her New Year's Eve celebrating pulled up in front of the building.

It was not the first time Lorna and Sally had seen each other since Philip moved out of the building, but it was the first time Lorna had seen

Sally with a man since then, and the first time she had ever seen Sally drunk.

It was not an attractive sight.

Sally's blond hair, which she always wore up in a French knot, had come partially undone. Her lipstick was smeared. Her escort, a considerably younger man with bad skin, a receding hairline, and a paunch that was apparent even though he was wearing a loose-fitting top coat, was equally tipsy. Both of them were sporting conical-shaped party hats that fastened beneath their chins with rubber bands.

"Why, if it isn't Ms. Lorna Robinson," Sally said. "Fancy meeting you here!"

"Why?" Lorna asked. "We live in the same building."

"How *are* you," Sally gushed.

"I'm fine."

"Hap–py New Year!" the drunken young man said.

"Happy New Year."

"How is that dear ex-husband of yours?" Sally asked. She turned to the man at her side; her arm was linked through his, holding on to support herself. "Lorna has the *dearest* ex-husband," she said to him before returning her attention to Lorna. There was one of the most malicious smiles Lorna had ever seen on Sally's face.

"Welcome to the crowd," the man said to Lorna. *"Every* woman *I* go out with has an ex-husband."

Sally threw back her head, cackled a forced laugh, and hit the man lightly on the sleeve in response to his remark.

He hit her back in return, without pulling his

punch, a gesture which brought drunken tears to Sally's eyes.

"Hey, that hurt!" she said. "That really hurt!"

"Sorry," the man said, leering and rolling his eyes. "I guess I just don't know my own strength." This last remark was uttered in an affected tone that reminded Lorna of a 1930s gangster movie.

The pain of the punch seemed to clear Sally's head a bit. Suddenly, she caught sight of herself in the mirrors lining the lobby. One hand flew to her hair; the other attempted to repair her lipstick. Her expression changed. She looked hard at her companion, at the hat on his head, the leer that was still on his face; her eyes darted first to the front door and then to the elevator indicator, which showed a rapid approach to the lobby.

The elevator stopped and the door opened.

The man took Sally's arm firmly and led her into it. "It's the penthouse, you said, didn't you?" He suddenly sounded absolutely sober. He pushed the button for the penthouse floor, then turned to face Sally. He walked her up against the back of the elevator and imprisoned her there with the bulk of his body.

Lorna remained standing in the lobby.

"Good night, Sally," Lorna said pleasantly as the door began to close. "I'm going to wait for the next one."

Chapter Fifteen

THE NEW YEAR STARTED OUT COLD AND CLEAR, with two days of bright sun and nearly no wind. On the day before both Len and Philip and the children were to return to New York, however, a heavy storm blew in from Canada, leaving nearly eleven inches of snow in its wake which disrupted all transportation and closed the airports.

Lorna was surprised that this unexpected occurrence felt like a reprieve although she missed Len, *needed* him, and was looking forward to giving him the Christmas present she had bought for him.

It felt like a reprieve because, although she had accepted the dinner invitation without hesitation, Lorna was actually nervous about her Friday night date with Mike Bishop. What made her nervous was the unexpected realization that Mike Bishop was an *eligible* man and his behavior New Year's Eve had made it quite clear that he was not interested in a simple sexual relationship but in something more than that—something very much more than that—something that no one had wanted from her in a long time.

Somehow, in retrospect, Lorna found Mike's eligibility threatening. Even though Len was going to be late returning from Colorado, the snow-storm did have the potential of delaying Lorna's date with Mike, putting a decision off for a while—as well as delaying Philip's return with the children. So she welcomed the respite.

The apartment was desperately empty without Cindy and Daniel, but Lorna was also nervous about seeing Philip, as nervous as she had been about seeing Len again after their first meeting. But it was the nervousness about Mike that seemed to be the greatest because Lorna realized that, if Len didn't arrive before her date with Mike, the recent absence of satisfying lovemaking in her life was going to provide still another complication on Friday night.

On the first day of the storm, after consultation with Mr. Willet, Lorna did not even attempt to open the store although she did make the necessary calls to insure that the snow would be removed from the sidewalk in the area that was their responsibility. On the second day, there was business as usual, but no customers. Philip had called from Florida, letting her know that he and the children would be delayed at least until Friday, but she had not heard from either Mike Bishop or Len.

By late Friday morning, Lorna was convinced that her date with Mike Bishop was off, and she was annoyed with herself for her seesawing attitude. She had been nervously awaiting his call for several days but, now that he seemed to have forgotten, she was angry. Early in the afternoon, soon after she returned from her lunch break, she received a call from Mike at the store.

"Hi. I should have called earlier, but it didn't make any sense until I knew if the weather was going to clear," he said by way of greeting.

"That's okay," Lorna said. "But how did you get my number here?"

"I tracked you down through Beth. I hope you don't mind my calling you at work."

"No. This is fine," Lorna said. "We haven't had a customer in nearly forty-eight hours except for one frantic young writer who had run out of bond paper."

"Are we still on for tonight?"

"I don't know what to say," Lorna said. "I thought you had forgotten, and it's pretty hard getting around."

"I didn't forget," Mike said, "and I can manage."

"It's not only that," Lorna said. "There's at least a possibility that my ex-husband and children might get a flight through today. The airports are supposed to open this afternoon, and if they do, I'd like to be home."

"I understand that," Mike said. "Look, Lorna, I'd really like to see you tonight. What if I pick up some groceries and we have dinner at your place? That way, you'd be home if your children do come. I'll leave if that happens."

"Okay," Lorna said. "That sounds all right."

"Good," Mike said. "What time is convenient?"

"I'll expect you any time after seven-thirty."

"Wonderful, I'll see you then."

But it was Len, not Philip, who called on Friday night while Mike was at the apartment. He had left Margot and his children in Colorado for a few days, managed a flight to Philadelphia, and taken a train to Penn Station.

Although Lorna was having a pleasant evening, was, in fact, enjoying Mike's company because it was low-keyed and carried no responsibility, the opportunity to spend a night with Len was one she was not about to pass up. So, after asking Len to delay his arrival until eleven o'clock, she lied to Mike, told him that the call was from Philip and that he and her children were on the way in from the airport. She asked if he would mind leaving.

Mike was understanding; he left at ten-thirty after Lorna ordered a cab to make sure he could get home. They made arrangements to meet again the following week for dinner and, perhaps, a movie. This time, Lorna agreed more to hasten Mike's departure than from pleasure.

While she waited for Len, Lorna hastily cleaned up the table and kitchen, erasing signs of Mike's presence in the apartment. She took a fast second shower and changed into a dressing gown she had been saving for an occasion. It was peach-colored, floor-length, and had a lace ruff that ran from the neck to the waist, which was enhanced with a lace rose that served as the fastener for the belt. It was very flattering, skillfully cut, and tailored to accentuate the lines of her breasts and waist, falling from the belt to the floor in graceful folds that flowed around her thighs each time she took a step. It was the sexiest garment Lorna had ever owned, one she had bought for herself during the interim between Philip's confession of his involvement with Sally Thornton and her own decision to seek a divorce instead of attempting a reconciliation.

She had brushed her hair four times; checked her makeup even more often. She had paced the living room, even washed the kitchen sink with Windex.

At twelve minutes after eleven, the bell to Lorna's apartment rang.

Len had acquired a beautiful even deep tan on the ski slopes at Aspen, and he had taken off a pound or two although the loss had not been necessary. Carrying his skis under one arm, his hands occupied with two pieces of carry-on luggage, he stood in the doorway to Lorna's apartment. There was a broad smile on his handsome face at the sight of her although he looked very tired. Lorna experienced a surge of pleasure at Len's obvious eagerness to see her again, an eagerness that he made no attempt to hide.

Lorna took the bag from his left hand.

"Hey," she said. "This is heavier than I thought!"

"You chose wrong," Len said. "My right hand is much stronger. I carry the heavier bag in my left to try to strengthen it."

Somehow, they managed to get through the awkwardness of getting Len's things into the apartment and his coat off. Then she was in his arms, sighing from deep inside, the misgivings she had about their affair dissipated by the strength of their present passion. The feel of his body was a justification for everything, an affirmation of life. A pocket of heat surrounded her, a sense of safety that was experienced nowhere but in Len's arms, even though a different and equally strong sense of safety was known to her during embraces with Philip. . . .

She pulled away, drawing back into the circle of Len's arms, looking up at his face.

Both of them opened their mouths to speak, and neither of them said a word.

They exchanged smiles that originated from internal desires that each recognized as identical in the other.

They laughed.

Len bent and kissed Lorna first on the right, then the left, cheek.

"How about offering a weary traveler a drink?" he asked. "It was a long journey getting here."

"Okay," Lorna said. Surprisingly, as Lorna walked to the bar and poured them each cognacs, she thought that Philip wouldn't have asked her for a drink; he would have led her by the hand into the bedroom, already beginning to unbutton his shirt. There was no need for her to decide on a preference; it was enough simply to be aware of the difference. Which one would Mike be more like, she wondered, even more surprisingly, as a sudden and completely unexpected thought of him invaded her consciousness.

"I like your robe, Lorna," Len said. "You're looking wonderful. Your tan's flattering. You must have had a good time in Florida."

"I did. Got in plenty of sun and swimming and ate a lot of oranges. Played cards. Got things patched up with my ex-mother-in-law."

"I had a good time, too, but I missed you."

Len got up and met Lorna as she returned to the couch carrying two glasses of cognac. One hand reached for the back of her head so she could not escape his kiss; the other sought the vee between her legs. He swallowed her sigh; she cursed the glasses in her hands, which kept her arms from holding him closer. A part of her mind was preoccupied and she was unable to enjoy fully the magnificent rush of pleasure which he was arousing in her body. Her tongue darted to meet his; his suddenly became immobile, forcing her own to flirt, to act the coquette. A laugh from great delicious amusement bubbled up in her.

Len released her from the kiss, from the velvet snare, holding her by the shoulders now, holding her away from him.

"You're a minx, Lorna, did you know that?"

Then he took the glasses from her, placed them on the coffee table, turned her around, and propelled her into the bedroom.

How was it possible that she was so open for the heat of his mouth so quickly?

Some part of her, attempting to protect something she could not define, fought against the pleasure.

Then she yielded.

There was no choice.

No choice at all.

"Why wouldn't you marry me, Lorna?" Len asked. He was holding her to him, spoonlike, and the warmth of his breath caused the skin above her ear to tingle.

"I didn't like your attitude about children."

Len turned over on his back and sat up. He drew Lorna toward him. "You answered that question as if you were prepared for it," he said.

Lorna sat up. She turned around on the bed to face him, drawing her legs up and tucking her chin between her knees.

"Not really," she said. "But I talked about that with my friend Beth not too long after I started seeing you again."

"I'm not sure if it upsets me or flatters me that you've been talking about me."

Lorna shrugged. "I talked with Beth because I needed to get things straightened out in my own mind," she said. "Maybe it sounds hard, but it really didn't have nearly as much to do with you as it did with my own needs."

"What do you mean?"

"I was very confused after we saw each other that first day in Willet's—after I left you sitting on the library steps. I was much more upset than I think you realized."

Len was silent for some time. Lorna got restless. She rose from the bed, went to the living room, and got the cognac Len had taken from her earlier.

"Thanks," Len said as she handed him the glass.

Lorna got back in bed, this time leaning against the pillows so that she and Len were side by side. She had a feeling of satisfaction she had never known with Len before. The level of their love-making and this honest talk between them was helping her to bring their affair into perspective. "Unfinished business"—that's what Len had said back in October when they remet. Yes. That's what this was all about. Unfinished business.

"I think I know what you mean about my

attitude where children are concerned," Len said then. "I was really still a child myself when I was a teenager, but I thought it was smart to put kids down."

"Yes, you certainly did."

"I remember once saying something that got you very upset."

"What was that?"

"I said I thought all children should be kept in zoos until they were fourteen."

Lorna laughed. "It was just an overall attitude I remember," she said. "I don't recall your saying that!"

"Well, I did," Len said. "I read it somewhere, although I can't remember the source of the quote now."

"It's easy to pick up a snappy line from a book and use it even if it's not what you really think," Lorna said. "I think everybody's done that one time or other in their lives."

"I suppose so," Len said.

"You know what sticks in my mind?"

"What?" Len asked.

"Most of all, I remember the look on your face one time when we were at Marilen's house. Her older sister came over unexpectedly for a visit. She was due to have her first baby any day."

"I remember," Len said. "She was so big! She put my hand on her stomach, and I could feel the baby move. It was so big! I looked at you and tried to imagine what it would be like if you were carrying a baby that big, and . . . it frightened me," Len said. "I didn't realize how much it frightened me until Margot and I had our first child. I realized that I had considered the possibility that she might die in childbirth and, if she did, I would be responsible."

"Are you serious?"

"Yes, of course I am," Len said. "But that knowledge was actually a relief. What wasn't a relief was that I thought about you the day Margot had our first son. I'm sure that fear must have influenced the way I spoke about having children to you, even though I didn't understand it then. The whole thing, the birth process, it's so scary, so mysterious. . . ." Len broke off. He took a large swallow of the cognac, nearly draining the glass, held it up to observe it, then finished it.

"Refill?" Lorna asked.

"Okay."

Back and forth they talked, opening to each other, exchanging thoughts, filling in what they could about things the years had taught them. It seemed easier for Len to accept the notion that Lorna hadn't married him because of his attitude about children and for fear of her own sexuality than for Lorna to accept the idea that Len's fear of having children was an instinctive fear for her life.

At one point, feeling weary, Lorna was prompted to glance at the bedside clock. "Ye gads," she said. "Four-thirty in the morning. It sure seems like a strange hour to be holding existential conversations about life and childbirth."

And it was at that moment they heard a key click in the lock of the door of the apartment.

With no time to prepare, no time to do anything at all but pull the blankets around them, suddenly Lorna found herself naked in bed with a man who was a stranger to the two red-eyed exhausted children who stood in the doorway of her bedroom with their father behind them.

"God, Beth," Lorna said late that afternoon. "I didn't even get a chance to give Len the present I bought him for Christmas. I'm not sure I've ever experienced such an awkward moment unless it was later in the morning when we all sat down at the table to have breakfast together. Philip was exhausted and he had spent the rest of the night sleeping on the couch."

"I had Dawn walk in on me one night," Beth said, "but Bert wasn't standing behind her the way Philip was behind your kids. That makes a difference."

"Yes," Lorna said. "That made it even harder."

"What did you do?"

"I said, 'Hello, kids. Would you mind closing the door and getting yourselves right into bed? I'm not dressed, and I'll talk to you in the morning after everyone wakes up. I'm glad to see you. Happy New Year!'"

Beth chuckled. "And what did they do?"

Daniel turned away without saying anything and went right into Philip's arms for a hug. Cindy said 'Happy New Year!' then she began to smile, *winked* at me, and closed the door."

"Did Philip say anything?"

"Sure. He ignored me completely and said, 'Hello, Marsh. How are things at good old Brockton and Company?'"

Beth laughed heartily and, despite herself, Lorna joined in.

"You're right," Lorna said, "it really was funny. But it was Cindy's reaction that affected me most. I asked her about that just before I came up here, and she said the strangest thing."

"What was that?" Beth asked.

"She said, 'It made me feel funny but also really good to see you with him.' I asked her why, and you know what my wonderful daughter said?"

"What?"

"She said, 'Until that moment, I'd always thought of you just as my mother. Len's a really handsome man. As handsome as Daddy. Now I think of you as a woman, too.'"

Chapter Sixteen

IN THE MIDDLE OF JANUARY, LOOKING AHEAD TO HER sixtieth birthday which fell on Saint Valentine's Day, Mildred called and suggested that she come visit Lorna and the children to celebrate the occasion.

Lorna agreed, trying hard to sound enthusiastic about the visit. She hadn't seen her mother for nearly five months, one of the longest hiatuses in her life during which they had not had a face-to-face meeting.

The impending visit, though it was nearly a month away, sent Lorna into a frenzy of housecleaning. Although it played havoc with her budget, she borrowed Willemina from Beth for a day, and hired her for a second. The kitchen cabinets were cleared of their stores of produce, the shelves washed, the cans dusted, things replaced in the best possible order. Every closet was examined. One Saturday, Lorna even rented suitable machinery and cleaned the rugs.

She continued to see Len several times a week. At first she was surprised and disappointed, but then resigned, when she realized that the level of intimacy they had achieved during the evening he had returned to New York might never again be shared between them. There was simply no time for confidences during their midday meetings, no time for anything but their lovemaking.

Lorna had dinner dates with Mike Bishop on several occasions as well. He was a pleasant man but his obvious need to find a wife to replace the one he had lost bothered her. Furthermore, Cindy seemed confused because Lorna was dating a man different from the one with whom she had seen her in bed. Although Mike had made a few verbal thrusts toward her, he usually attempted nothing more than a friendly good-night kiss. Lorna had lost her desire to sleep with him as a means of comparing his techniques with Len's lovemaking.

She finally told Mike without mincing words that she could see no future in their continuing to date. Mike was not happy about her decision, but Lorna stuck to it.

Her frequent conversations with Beth helped her to sort out her thoughts. Lorna accepted without question Beth's observation that the taking of a lover, married or not, caused a change in the way that a woman viewed herself. A lover made a woman feel more attractive; therefore, she *was* more attractive, and this helped her attract other eligible men.

But what bothered Lorna, and what Beth could not help her with, was the seemingly obvious fact that Lorna really didn't want an eligible man in her life just then.

The third weekend in January Philip was to have the children with him. However, for the first time since their divorce, Philip called and asked to be released from his bi-monthly obligation.

"It doesn't matter if you say yes or no," Philip said. "I just can't this weekend. Please explain to the kids. I'll make it up to them and to you at the end of next month or the beginning of March. I just can't have them right now. That's all."

"All right, Philip," Lorna agreed.

"Thanks," Philip said. "I appreciate your not asking questions too."

"No. I understand. Take care of yourself, Philip," Lorna said. "I know you're finishing the new book."

"Yes," Philip replied.

For a long moment after Philip hung up, Lorna held the phone receiver in her hand, staring at it. She wasn't angry because she hadn't made plans for the weekend. But Philip had sounded distracted and depressed. She had lived through similar moods of his before. Once, when he was finishing one of his books, Philip had jokingly said that completing an involved and time-consuming creative project was the closest a man could ever come to experiencing what a woman went through during pregnancy. Lorna believed there was some truth in the statement.

At the tail end of January, a belated January thaw brought fifty-degree weather to New York. The break lasted for nearly ten days. There was a noticeable upsurge of business at Willet's. Lorna still missed Gail's presence in the store, but was pleased that Gail was happy in the situation that Bert Pilsner had found for her in one of his Queens stores. Business at Willet's had begun to pick up. The line of leather goods which Mr. Willet had authorized Lorna to try out the previous fall was proving financially successful much to her relief. Even more important, Cindy's second-quarter report card, received the first week in February, showed an overall improvement, bearing out Lorna's theory that backstopping her daughter's assignments was a step in the right direction. Further, when Mildred's visit had caused Lorna to do a thorough housecleaning, Cindy had remarked that she wanted to have a good report card to show her grandmother.

Like Lorna, Mildred did not particularly care for airplanes, so she chose instead to take the train from Buffalo to New York.

For a woman who was within days of entering her sixth decade of life, Mildred was an exceptionally attractive woman who had maintained her youthful appearance for the last thirty years. She wore her slightly wavy hair short and moderately fluffed. She did not color her hair, but the gray had blended well with her natural dark-ash blond.

Her clothes were stylish, although they were generally made of easy-care polyester, and she leaned to browns and beiges as "her" colors.

Mildred did not "look her age"; she had the ageless look of a mature woman who took care of herself. However, except for walking, exercise played no part in her daily routine.

"Cindy—Daniel—I'm glad to see you," Mildred said, suffering her grandchildren's hugs. Mildred was not one for showing physical affection. "Lorna, you're looking very well. You've taken off weight."

"A pound or two, maybe," Lorna said, "but I haven't been working at it. I've been just about the same weight for years. You know that. And you're looking well, too, Mother."

Mildred shrugged out of her coat, which she gave to Cindy to hang in the closet. Daniel took her suitcase and overnight bag into Lorna's bedroom where she would stay during her visit. Lorna had made room for her mother's dresses and other hangables in the closet, and she had cleaned out a drawer in the dresser. She would sleep on the sofa bed in the den during her mother's visit.

For the first half hour or so after Mildred arrived, Cindy and Daniel hovered around, paying tribute to her, getting her a cup of coffee. They looked proud when Mildred complimented them on their choice of Christmas presents. They boisterously opened the presents Mildred had brought with her instead of sending them in December—a sweater she had knitted for Daniel which fit perfectly and a dozen comic books and movie magazines for Cindy. These were so untypical a present for Mildred to have chosen, and yet so appropriate for Cindy, that Lorna felt a strange pang she could not identify.

Was it because Mildred had never once given her a present which was appreciated as much as this simple one was by Cindy? Or because her mother had made a sweater for Daniel but had never knitted a sweater for her?

But there was a sweater for Lorna, too. It was beautiful, a soft light-blue cashmere pullover—a sweater that delighted Lorna. She would have exclaimed about it with the same joy Cindy and Daniel had expressed if she had received her present before her children had received theirs.

Soon Cindy and Daniel deserted the living room in favor of the television set in the den, and Lorna and Mildred were left alone. As usual, Mildred had chosen to sit in the wing chair that faced away from the windows. Lorna sat on the couch. The snow which had fallen early in January had melted during the thaw later in the month, and February had so far proved to be extremely cold, leaving no doubt that the city was in the throes of winter. But there had been no additional snowfall. Except for the leafless trees, the vista from the windows was identical to the one Lorna had seen at the end of the previous year. She stared at the view for so long that Mildred craned herself around in the wing chair and also looked out the window.

"Is something happening on the river?" Mildred asked.

"No," Lorna said. "I was just looking at the view, that's all. It's one of the things I like best about this apartment."

"Yes," Mildred agreed. "It's very nice."

During the weeks since Mildred had called to

invite herself to New York to celebrate her birth-day, Lorna had given considerable thought to telling her mother that she was seeing Len Gold again. But until Mildred was actually in the apartment, she had not made a decision. Now, facing her mother, Lorna knew that she was not going to tell her about Len's reappearance in her life. It would serve no purpose other than to incite a feud between them.

"Are you hungry, Mom, or was the coffee enough? Would you like a second cup? I can give you some cake to go with it, or a sandwich, or we could have supper early."

"No, please," Mildred said. "Don't bother. I'm sure I'll be perfectly comfortable with whatever kind of a routine you have established for yourself. But if you don't mind, I'd like to take a look around to see if you've changed the apartment."

"Sure, make yourself at home."

Mildred got up from the chair then and went on a tour of the apartment. She went into every room, even opening the utility closet door in the hallway before returning to the living room and sitting down again. There was a pleasant smile on her face which made Lorna feel good although she did not know why.

"You weren't a particularly neat child, Lorna," Mildred said. Lorna could feel herself groan inwardly. "But you've turned into a very good housekeeper. And I like the looks of my grandchildren, too. I don't get a chance to tell you this often, but I love you very much and I'm proud of you."

"Thank you, Mom," Lorna said, enormously

pleased. Her mother's comments had been unexpected and the words touched a place in Lorna which needed exactly that gratification at exactly that moment.

"All I did was tell you the truth," Mildred said.

"Well, thank you again. It really means a lot to me."

Yes, Lorna thought, it did mean a lot to her, even if it didn't make up for something else that was lacking, something she couldn't even begin to define.

Because it gave her pleasure to do so and because she rarely had the opportunity any longer, Lorna spent several days planning and cooking for the small celebration which was to occur on Mildred's birthday. For dessert she chose a whipped-cream-topped chocolate cake baked from a recipe which had been Lorna's grandmother's. It was a moist heavy cake that improved with a day's rest in the refrigerator. Mildred had baked the cake each year for Lorna's birthday until she was sixteen; now it was Lorna's turn to pass the recipe on to Cindy. Lorna made the cake secretly in Beth's apartment, with Cindy gleefully helping, and left it in Beth's refrigerator overnight.

Although she was reluctant to do so, Lorna acceded to Mildred's wishes and asked Philip to join them for the Sunday birthday dinner. Beth and Dawn were also invited. Lorna set a separate table for the three children in the den so they wouldn't miss a television special, and served the four adults at the dinner table in the dining alcove.

This evening was the first time that Lorna and

Philip had been together since her Florida trip, unless she counted the night when he had found her in bed with Len and the following morning. Despite their custody agreement, and in a completely uncharacteristic mood, Philip had canceled out a second weekend during which he was to have taken Cindy and Daniel. Although the children seemed to miss him, and called him more often on the telephone than they normally did, neither had voiced a protest about this change in their schedule. They, too, were used to a change in Philip's mood when he was completing a book. Lorna had not considered the possibility that Philip's motivation in canceling out the weekends might have to do with anything other than his work.

Philip arrived exactly on time, ringing the doorbell instead of using the key Lorna had let him keep in case of emergency.

Lorna opened the door, and was so startled that she did not even make a comment other than a polite greeting.

Philip had lost nearly ten pounds, ten pounds which he could ill afford. There were deep shadows beneath his eyes, and he had let a scheduled haircut go by.

"Jesus," Beth said to Philip when he came into the living room, "you're looking lousy. What's up?"

"I'm working too hard and thinking too much," he said, "and I'm having a lot of trouble with the book."

Mildred had gotten up from the wing chair when Philip entered the room. He hugged her and gave her an affectionate kiss on each cheek. "I'm really glad to see you, Mildred," he said.

"Yes, I'm glad to see you, too. But Beth's right. You're looking terrible."

Philip shrugged again. "I guess I just don't have anyone to take care of me now," he said, glancing at Lorna, who headed to the kitchen to finish last-minute dinner preparations without responding to Philip's remark. There was in her, suddenly, a terrible certainty that it wasn't Philip's work that was bothering him at all—a premonition that was borne out almost immediately after she served the first course and sat at the table.

"Did Lorna tell you that she's been seeing Len Gold, Mildred?" Philip asked.

"No. No, she didn't tell me that." Mildred looked hard at Philip, cocking her head to one side before turning her attention to Lorna. She stared at her daughter silently, a host of unspoken questions apparent on her face and in her eyes.

"That's right," Lorna said. "I didn't mention it, but Philip's right. I bumped into Len unexpectedly late last fall, and we've been seeing a bit of each other."

The sound Philip made was not unlike the sound of clearing his throat, but it carried a harsh tone of sardonic amusement that left no doubt in anyone's mind at the table, not even Mildred's, that Lorna's remark was a serious understatement.

"That wasn't necessary, Philip," Lorna said, her voice tight and controlled, her anger so close to the surface she was not sure she would be able to contain it.

"What wasn't necessary, Lorna?" Philip asked.

"Bringing up the subject you just did, or your snort as an editorial comment, either."

"Come on, you two," Beth said, nervously

149

pushing the remains of her appetizer around on her plate with her fork and trying to change the subject. "Have you been doing anything since you've been here, Mildred? Getting out, or doing any shopping? There's a store just a few blocks away that's having a sale, and—"

"I was sure you'd tell Mildred about Len first thing, Lorna," Philip persisted. "I know how much she used to like him, you told me that, and the morning when we all had breakfast here, he mentioned to me how much he'd always liked *you*, Mildred."

Lorna pushed back from the table and stood up. "Get out, Philip!" she said. "Get out of here, right now! I don't know what you could possibly be thinking of, but you have no right—"

"No right? Are you saying that I don't have the right to hold up my end of a polite conversation at this dinner table? If that's the case, why did you invite me?"

"I invited you because Mildred asked me to."

Philip spread his hands imploringly, addressing himself to Mildred. "You don't want me to leave, do you, Mildred?" he asked. "I practically just got here."

"Sit down, Lorna," Mildred said. "And, no, I don't want you to leave, Philip. What I want is to know what's going on here."

"Why, nothing. Nothing at all," Philip said.

"What do you mean, 'nothing at all?'" Lorna's voice rose despite her attempt to control herself. "How dare you, Philip?"

"How dare I *what?*" Philip said, his voice rising also. "All I did was let your mother know that you're doing just what I was doing with Sally Thornton. That got you angry enough so you insisted on a separation and divorce. Well, this business with Len gets me angry, too, except that there's nothing I can do about it!"

Philip was shouting now. Suddenly Dawn, Daniel, and Cindy were in the dining alcove.

"Hey, what's going on?" Daniel demanded.

"Nothing!" Philip shouted.

"Nothing!" Lorna shouted.

"Cindy," Mildred said, "are you all right? You're looking very pale."

"No, Grandma, I'm not. My stomach's been feeling funny today, and I've got the strangest crampy feeling. . . ." Cindy left then, heading for the bathroom.

"Maybe you'd better go see if she's all right, Lorna," Mildred said.

"Yes. Yes. That's a good idea."

"Go on back to the den, kids," Beth said.

"No, I want to stay here for a little while," Daniel said. "I don't feel so good, either. I don't like it when people fight. It gets me upset." His breathing sounded a little wheezy.

"Are you all right, Daniel?" Philip asked. "You're not having an asthma attack are you?"

"No, no, I don't think so," Daniel answered.

Lorna headed for the bathroom after giving a concerned glance at her son. "Keep an eye on him, Philip," she said.

"Yes, of course."

The bathroom door was shut. Lorna knocked. "Are you all right, Cindy-Bear?"

There was silence on the other side of the door.

Lorna knocked again. "Cindy? Cindy?"

Cindy opened the door.

She was sitting on the commode.

"Mom!" she said, a sense of wonder in her voice. "Mom! I think I've got my first period!"

———◄ ►———

Chapter Seventeen

CINDY'S GOT HER FIRST PERIOD," LORNA SAID when she returned to the dining alcove. "I should have been prepared, but I'm not. I'll have to make a trip to the drugstore."

"What's a 'period?'" Daniel asked.

Lorna glanced at Mildred, seeking help, but Mildred avoided her eyes and stared at her food which was now quite cold.

"You tell him, Philip," Lorna said. She headed for the closet and put on her coat. "Come with me, would you, Beth? And Mildred, would you go and stay with Cindy?"

"I . . . why don't I come with you and let Beth wait with Cindy?" Mildred suggested.

"No," Lorna said firmly. "No. You handled this situation very badly once. Try to do better this time, okay?"

Beth got up from the table and also got her coat.

"What's a 'period?'" Daniel asked Philip.

"It means she's a woman now," Dawn said.

"What's better, do you think?" Lorna asked Beth in the elevator. "Shall I start her out directly on tampons or sanitary napkins?"

"Why don't we get both, and then you can give her a choice?"

"That's a good idea. You know, she isn't upset at all. She seemed proud, in fact."

"Things are different from when we were growing up," Beth said. "There are better sex-education courses in the schools. There are ads in magazines and even on television for tampons and napkins . . . my mother was pretty good about it with me and I've talked about it with Dawn. She's looking forward to menstruation, too."

When they returned to the apartment, Philip and Daniel were in the den, and Mildred, Dawn, and Cindy were still in the bathroom.

Cindy had a childishly eager smile on her face when Lorna and Beth joined them, but Mildred was looking visibly upset.

"What did you mean when you said I handled things badly once?" Mildred asked after Lorna had tended to Cindy, showing her how to adjust the sanitary belt and napkin she decided to try for the time being. She left the decision about the use of tampons for later.

Lorna shrugged. "You never told me anything helpful about menstruation or sex, either, Mildred," Lorna said, although she knew Mildred disliked it when she called her by her first name. "Don't you remember? I didn't know what was happening at all when I got my first period, and your attitude made things even worse."

"What do you mean?"

"You made me feel as if there were something the matter with me. I'd forgotten that, or at least learned to live with it."

"What do you expect from me anyway, Lorna?" Mildred said then, showing unusual spunk. "I'm the way I am because that's the way I was taught by my mother."

"Yes, of course, I can understand that, but—"

"No, young lady," Mildred said. "You obviously don't understand. You never knew your grandmother. I loved her very much, but I hated her, too, because she was uneducated and old-fashioned, just like I know you think I am."

"I don't—"

"Yes, you do, Lorna. I know that. I've always known that—oh, not uneducated, because I'm not, but old-fashioned, yes, and maybe you're right about that. But I'm nothing compared to my mother, who grew up in the old country and never even learned how to speak English properly. It's one of the shames of my life that when my mother died the first reaction I felt—the first reaction I could identify—was relief."

"You don't mean that!"

"Yes. Yes, I do."

Cindy came into the living room with Dawn. "Gad," she said, "Dad and Daniel won't let us into the den. Dad says they're having a 'man-to-man' talk in there." She flounced down on the sofa.

Mildred turned to Cindy. "You know," she said, "when I was a little girl, we used to use clean rags and cotton when we had a period. There weren't any such things as sanitary napkins or tampons."

"You're kidding!" Cindy said.

"No. No, I'm not," Mildred said, although her eyes were on Lorna. "And lots of women used to die in childbirth. Things were much more frightening then than they are now."

Lorna shifted uncomfortably on the couch.

Cindy's hands went to her stomach. "I'm feeling strange," she said.

"Yes, yes, of course, you are," Beth said. "You're having a new experience. New experiences often feel strange. Dawn, why don't you get Cindy an aspirin?"

"Okay," Dawn said.

"Do you want to go lie down for a while, Cindy?" Lorna asked.

"No. I'm feeling okay now that I know what's happening, but we'll leave you guys alone. Come on," she said to Dawn when she brought the aspirin. "Let's go to my room. Grandma brought me some new comics and a whole pile of movie magazines!"

"Okay!" Dawn said.

"Look, do you two want to be alone for a while?" Beth said to Lorna and Mildred when the girls were gone. "It sounds like you've got some talking to do. There's some stuff I've got to do downstairs. Why don't I go back to my place for awhile? Give me a call when you're ready to serve the birthday cake, and I'll come on back up."

"Thank you, that's considerate," Mildred said, before Lorna could tell Beth to stay.

"See you later," Beth said, heading for the door.

"She's right, Lorna," Mildred said when they were alone. "Somehow, we've never really done the kind of talking that we should have done when you were younger. I'm not going to apologize for that. I've always done what I thought was right. I assure you, there's a good possibility that every incident you remember that made you angry with me is an incident about which I probably still feel guilty. Your children are old enough now for you to realize how difficult it is to be a parent."

"Yes," Lorna said. And then, because her feelings were so close to the surface, Lorna was suddenly struck by the memory which had come to her on the train ride back from Florida.

"When I was very young," she said, "I remember creeping into bed with you and Dad before he died. Once I said something about that to you and you said, 'No, you never did that. I would never allow a child to invade the privacy of the bedroom I shared with my husband.' Why did you lie about that?"

Mildred frowned. "I don't remember that at all," she said. "I'm sure I never said anything like that."

"Yes, you did."

"We used to let you come into our room all the time," Mildred said. "I've wondered why you've never mentioned it, except that you never talk about your father and never ask me about him, either. I can't imagine why I would have ever made such a remark."

"You did, though. I'm sure you did!"

"Did I, Lorna? Did I really? Are you sure it wasn't a conversation you had with yourself at a time when you were very angry with me for something else?"

"What do you mean?"

"For a long time after your father died, you were very angry, angry and confused about everything, and you directed a great deal of that anger towards me as if I were somehow responsible for his death."

"I wasn't aware of that," Lorna said.

"No, of course not. You were so young, Lorna. Younger than Cindy is now."

Lorna turned away, suddenly feeling lost and very unsure of herself. There was some truth in what Mildred had said. Her father's death had affected her greatly, so much that she had blocked his existence out of her consciousness, never thinking about him, never talking about "parents" but always just about Mildred. Was it possible that Mildred was right, that she had imagined the exchange of words between them?

Yes.

Yes, it was possible, in the same way that what Mildred had said earlier about her grandmother made sense to Lorna also.

On an impulse which she did not in the slightest try to restrain, Lorna got up from the couch and knelt on the floor by the side of the wing chair in which Mildred was sitting. She threw her arms around her mother's waist and gave her a hug.

"What can I say? What can I possibly say."

"You might try 'I love you,'" Mildred replied.

By the time dusk had fallen, there was a sense of the air having been cleared completely. Daniel and Philip had returned to the living room. Cindy had taken a rest and a short nap. Beth had returned to the apartment for the long overdue lighting of the candles and serving of the birthday cake. Philip's earlier mood had altered too. He apologized to Lorna, although he was unusually quiet and left almost immediately after they finished with the cake and coffee. Mildred was returning to Buffalo the following Tuesday, and Philip promised to resume his weekends with the children starting Friday.

Lorna was glad that Mildred had not asked her a single question about Len. However, she described the birthday party to Len when she saw him later in the week.

"Sounds like it was heavy," Len said. "A memorable birthday for Mildred, that's for sure."

"Yes. For Cindy, too. For all of us. I was very upset with Philip. I don't understand what prompted him at all."

"Don't you, Lorna?" Len asked. "Don't you really?"

His hands were on her breasts, hard and demanding, and his mouth came down on hers in a bruising kiss. "He still wants you, don't you realize that? But you're mine now, aren't you? Just the way you should have been years ago. Just the way you're going to be."

"What do you mean?"

"I've made a decision."

"About what?" Lorna asked, somehow knowing what Len was about to say, dreading the moment.

"I'm going to leave Margot," Len said then. "I'm going to leave her because you're going to marry me. You are going to marry me, aren't you, Lorna?" Again his mouth was on her, demanding, ordering her to say the word he wanted to hear when he pulled back to allow her to speak.

But she could not.

She had come close to anticipating such a moment as this in the past months, but she had always rejected the possibility that Len would actually make such a decision.

Had she known right along, and simply refused to accept it?

Was it possible she had known from the first day she had seen Len again in Willet's?

It didn't matter.

What mattered was that she knew with absolute certainty that she wanted nothing more from Len than she had now—nothing more than these sessions of passionate lovemaking.

She didn't want to marry him!

She didn't want to be his wife!

Slowly her head turned from side to side on the pillow, then faster and faster, and deep inside her brain a single word echoed: no, no, *no* . . . She had what she wanted from Len.

She was content with things the way they were.

Chapter Eighteen

WHAT WAS IT THAT MADE LORNA REALIZE HER affair with Len could not continue?

She wasn't sure herself.

It was at least a month before Len finally accepted without further questioning that she meant what she said, that she was not going to marry him if he left Margot. During this period, however, he called her several times a day at the store and asked for more and more of her time.

Still, she could not make herself say the words that would keep him away altogether.

Lorna was no longer seeing Mike Bishop, and could not tolerate the thought of returning to a life-style that did not include any intimacy at all. Yet Len's persistence was bothering her. In some way she did not understand, she knew that to continue seeing him was almost intolerable and that returning to a life without him was becoming more and more tempting.

After the night when Philip and the children had found her and Len in bed together, she had made no attempt to continue keeping the affair a secret from Daniel and Cindy. Occasionally, Len would come to the apartment for dinner, even staying overnight. Cindy accepted the situation quite casually now that Lorna was no longer dating Mike. But Daniel did not, and Lorna found herself faced with a rebellious son who, for the first time in his life, began to fight back at her. As Cindy had done earlier in the year, Daniel began to grow lax about his schoolwork. Even more ominous, early in March, Daniel had the first serious asthma attack he had had in over a year.

Lorna made a decision.

It was time to end things with Len.

She told him on a Friday late in March, during one of their lunchtime trysts. Philip was coming that day to pick up the children after school to take them for the weekend. Lorna had thought things through carefully, but had been unable to judge what Len's reaction would be, much less her own. She sensed that she would be able to deal with the changed situation better knowing that she would have a few days alone to sort things out in her mind.

Of all the possibilities that had occurred to her, the real situation proved to be one she had not thought of at all.

"I can't see you any more, Len," she said. "We can't go on like this."

Without a word, saying not a single word, asking not a single question, Len got up from the bed, dressed and left the apartment.

It seemed so easy, yet the silence in the bedroom after the front door of the apartment closed behind Len seemed to mock her. Slowly she dressed, too, and headed back to Willet's, glad that she was not going to be alone for the afternoon.

When she returned home from work that night, however, she was surprised to find Philip and the children still in the apartment. Normally, they were gone before she returned from work. Philip was on the telephone; he looked annoyed, and his greeting to Lorna was a barely perceptible nod.

"Go into the den for a while, kids, will you?" Philip asked after he hung up the phone abruptly.

"What's the matter, Philip?" Lorna asked.

"That was Len. He's drunk, and he demanded to speak to you. His tone was very belligerent. I didn't like it at all. He was furious that I was here and you weren't. What's happening?"

"Nothing, I—"

"Have you broken off with him?"

For a moment, although she didn't know why,

Lorna was tempted to lie, but she didn't. Instead, she told Philip the truth.

"Yes," Lorna said, "I've decided not to see him any more. I told him today. Earlier today. We saw each other at lunchtime."

"Why?" Philip asked.

"I can't see him any more. He wants to leave his wife and marry me, and I don't want that."

"You don't?"

"No, I don't," Lorna said. "Is that really such a surprise?"

"Yes. It is," Philip said. "I thought you were in love with him."

Lorna shrugged. "Maybe, in some sort of a way. But not the marrying way. I never wanted to marry him. I just wanted to know what it felt like to make love with him. Now I know, and it's exciting, but. . . ."

"That's the way I felt about Sally Thornton," Philip said.

"I realize that," Lorna said.

"Look, if you don't mind, I think I'll stick around for a while," Philip said. "Len's really drunk. I have a feeling he might come over instead of calling again, and I'm not sure you'll be able to handle him."

"Do you really think he might do that?"

"Yes, I do."

Lorna went to the kitchen and mixed Bloody Marys for Philip and herself, taking a little time to absorb the information. It was tempting to ask Philip to stay, but to do so carried the danger of intimacy. She wasn't really ready yet for that.

She made a decision.

She handed Philip the Bloody Mary she'd made for him.

They clinked glasses.

"I don't really think there's going to be any trouble," she said, "but it would be nice if you'd stay for a half hour or so just in case Len calls back."

"Fine," Philip said. "That sounds reasonable."

Lorna turned on the stereo, fiddling with the dial until she found a station playing mellow jazz standards. It reminded her of New Year's Eve and the easy-going dates she had had with Mike Bishop. But Philip was moved also to reminisce about the music, remembering aloud a dance they had attended years before when the same tune that was playing had been played by a live band.

For a second, Lorna thought Philip was going to ask her to dance; before he could do so, she moved purposefully away from him, finished her drink, and decisively put the glass on a table.

"Look," she said. "I've changed my mind. If Len calls on the phone there isn't any problem, and I can call the doorman and tell him not to let Len up if he comes here without calling first. That would do just as well."

"Yes," Philip said, somewhat reluctantly. "That would be all right." He finished his own drink. "I'll tell the doorman on our way out then, okay?"

"Yes. Thanks."

"You're welcome." Philip collected Cindy and Daniel and headed for the door. "We're not going away this weekend," he said. "If you need me—if there's trouble—give a call. Okay?"

"Sure," Lorna said.

"Promise?"

"I promise."

There was trouble.

At about eleven o'clock that night, after Lorna had hung up on Len three times, he showed up at the building and the doorman was unable to restrain him. For a full five minutes, Lorna huddled behind the front door while Len pounded on it with his fist. Finally, but only after both she and the doorman threatened to call the police, Len left. But he telephoned again at two in the morning and, again, the following morning at six.

"What am I going to do, Beth?" Lorna asked. "I wasn't afraid of Len before, but now I am."

"Did you call Philip? You told me he said you should do that if there was a problem."

"No, I didn't. It's really my business, not his, but I'm worried. Len hasn't called back since early this morning, but I'm afraid he's going to show up again."

"Do you want to stay here tonight? At my place?"

"No. Thanks for the offer, but I don't want to do that. I can't let him scare me out of my own apartment!"

"Maybe you should take the phone off the hook. At least that way you'd get a night's sleep."

"Yes, that's a good idea," Lorna said.

"What if I call Philip and tell him what happened?" Beth asked. "I can understand why it would be hard for you to do that."

"I don't know," Lorna said. "Use your own judgment, Beth, okay? I'm not sure that Philip wouldn't create as much of a problem as Len is creating."

"Well, I'll think about it before I do anything," Beth said. "And why don't you go and try to nap for a while? You look exhausted."

"I am."

It was still daylight when Lorna returned to her apartment. The phone was ringing. She let it ring, then took the receiver off the hook, closed the curtains in her bedroom, undressed, and got into bed. She had expected resistance from Len, but she had also expected him to act rationally, and it bothered her that she had so completely misjudged the situation.

She turned on her side, hugging the pillow. She could smell the smell of Len on the case, and unwanted memories began to plague her. Had she been cruel for a second time?

Perhaps.

Perhaps she had been.

Perhaps there was a way she could have softened the blow to Len for which he was obviously unprepared, but, if so, it had not occurred to her. Her intentions were self-protective, and she refused to allow herself to feel guilty.

No, she said to herself firmly. I'm not going to feel guilty about things this time.

We finished the unfinished business, and whatever else there might have been is over and done with.

It wasn't meant to be, and it isn't going to be.

With that thought firmly in mind, Lorna fell into a troubled sleep.

She was awakened by the sound of someone in

the living room, of the door to the apartment being gently closed.

Had she imagined it, or did her heart skip a beat?

How did Len get a key?

Had he taken the spare key during one of his visits to the apartment?

Why hadn't he used it last night?

She closed her eyes, realizing that she was nearly immobilized with fear.

She had left the bedroom door ajar. The sound of it being pushed open caused her to open her eyes.

Philip was standing in the doorway.

He crossed to the bed—the first time he had been in the bedroom with her since their separation—and sat by her side.

"Beth called," he said. "I thought I'd better come over. I tried calling, but the line was busy for nearly an hour. I got worried."

Lorna sat up. A laugh of relief escaped her. "I took the phone off the hook. I heard you in the living room," she said, "and I thought it was Len. I got scared."

"I can see," Philip said. His hand reached out and came to rest between her breasts. "Your heart is beating very fast."

"I don't like being scared," Lorna said. "It's a terrible feeling."

But she wasn't afraid any more! Philip was there, the way he had been when they were married. She sat up and her arms opened to him of their own volition. She buried her head against his shoulder. "Hold me," she said. "Please hold me. Hold me. Don't let me go."

"I didn't want to let you go, Lorna."

"I know. I know."

"Do you? Do you know how much I love you? How much I've always loved you? Do you know how much I want you? Do you know?"

"No," Lorna said, drawing them both back against the pillow. "Show me."

"What's the matter, Lorna?" Philip was leaning on an elbow. The bedroom was comfortably warm, but apparently some need for the continued feel of contact on his skin made Philip pull the quilt around him. Suddenly he had a look that reminded Lorna of Daniel dealing with an uncooperative sleeping bag.

Lorna smiled; some need of her own for continued contact made her run her tongue across the length of Philip's still exposed shoulder.

"I'm always quiet after making love," she said, the words unexpectedly provoking a strong echo of the past in her mind.

"Yes, you are."

A sense of *déjà vu* overwhelmed her. But when the same dialogue had been exchanged between her and Len, she had not been tempted to share her thoughts about the mystery of the differences of bodies as she suddenly, desperately, wanted to do with this man she loved.

Something held her back.

It was, somehow, she knew, a watershed situation, a moment in time capable of altering much of what would come after. Yet it was Philip, not she, who spoke first.

"This was different. There was something different about the feelings."

"Yes." There was in her an overwhelming gratitude that Philip knew she needed just those words at exactly that moment.

"Strange, isn't it? I thought I knew your body, everything there was to know about it." Slowly he gathered the quilt away from her; traced a finger through the valley between her breasts. His hand came to rest on the curve of her stomach. "You've had my children."

"Our children."

His laugh came from the place where pain and pleasure make their uneasy marriage. "Can't you just see a character in my situation directing his love to a lady who does not show the signs of that?" he said. Taking his time, prolonging the moment beyond the bearable, he looked at her, at her body, then with a groan his hands reached for her breasts—they were so much fuller now than they had been when she was his virgin bride!—and his cheek and mouth sought to erase the marks pregnancies had left elsewhere as reminders.

Momentarily, this unexpected display of passion felt to Lorna like an attack, and involuntarily her muscles tightened, refusing to respond to her mind's voice which beseeched her to accept her man's love.

Her man!

Her mate!

"I love you!" Was that her voice defining the parameters of their space? Her voice articulating the exact feelings they shared at that moment?

But his lips were on hers then, and she was never to know.

Perhaps it had been his voice saying the words for them both.

ATTENTION ROMANCE FANS!

If you enjoyed this book and would like to receive a free subscription to Ballantine's Love & Life Romance Newsletter, fill out the coupon below. You'll get personal glimpses into romance authors' lives and work, and more news of new and unforgettable romantic reading from Ballantine.

LOVE & LIFE
Romance
Newsletter
for the woman who wants the most from love & life.

BALLANTINE BOOKS, Dept. Love & Life
201 E. 50th Street, New York, N.Y. 10022

Yes, please send me a free subscription to Ballantine's
Love & Life Romance Newsletter.

Name⎯⎯⎯⎯⎯⎯⎯⎯⎯⎯⎯⎯⎯⎯⎯⎯⎯⎯⎯⎯⎯

Address⎯⎯⎯⎯⎯⎯⎯⎯⎯⎯⎯⎯⎯⎯⎯⎯⎯⎯⎯

City⎯⎯⎯⎯⎯⎯⎯⎯⎯State⎯⎯⎯⎯Zip Code⎯⎯⎯⎯⎯